Books by Crissy Smith

Were Chronicles

I0684335

Pack Alpha
Pack Enforcer
Pack Territory
Pack Rogue
Pack Community
Pack Mates
Pack Daughter
Pack Hunter
Pack Council
Pack Security
Pack Beta
Pack Secrets
Pack Balance
Pack Investigator
Pack Law

Corporate Wolves

The Favour
Losing Control

Secrets

The Shifter and the Dreamer

Shifter Chronicles

Birds of Prey
Bear Claw
Eye of the Tiger

Coyote's Kiss
Wolf Pack

Bloodlines

Bite

Bite Me!

Savage Love

Summer Seductions

Summers' Girl

Cloaks and Daggers

Vampire Hunter

Lust Bites

Seduced by the Neighbour
Fated Love
Bid High
Lacey's Seduction

What's Her Secret?

Designated Alpha
Last Call

Single Titles

Eternal
Magical Ménage
Vamps in the City

Pack Alpha

ISBN # 978-1-78686-029-3

©Copyright Crissy Smith 2016

Cover Art by Posh Gosh ©Copyright 2016

Interior text design by Claire Siemaszkiewicz

Totally Bound Publishing

Were Chronicles

PACK ALPHA

CRISSY SMITH

Dedication

To my husband and daughter who let me be myself and
dream my dreams

Prologue

Cool wind whipped the fur around her face as she leapt over a log to land easily on her paws. She could smell the water from the creek ahead as well as the damp soil and other critters running around.

As she slowed down, her heart continued to beat frantically. Movement to her left drew her attention. A powerful male wolf stepped into view. She almost stumbled from the power that radiated from the shifter.

Instinct had her dropping down to her belly as the wolf strode toward her. She rested her chin on her front paws to show the appropriate amount of submission. She didn't want to challenge this male – no, indeed, her body was reacting to his dominance by tightening in arousal. He lowered his head while he was still several yards away and she got the distinct impression that he was scenting her.

She rolled over onto her back and tucked her paws close to her chest, showing him that she was completely open to him. When he finally reached her he used his snout to push her paws aside and nuzzled the soft vulnerable skin of her belly. She whimpered in both obedience and need. He rewarded her with a lick across her muzzle before he gave her side a strong push, causing her to roll.

He braced himself over her back and she knew what would come next. She lifted her rear end up into the air to accept him.

Marissa Boyd gasped as she was startled awake. She panted, turned on from her erotic dream, and her entire body flushed and hot. Fuck, that had been wild.

Next to her, the man she'd picked up at the bar the night before was snoring softly. Damn, she'd forgotten about him.

She climbed out of her king-sized bed quietly, hoping not to disturb her sleeping partner. Hell, she wished they had gone back to his place instead of hers, then she could have slipped away without having to face him again. Instead, she was going to have to do the whole 'Good morning, had a great time, don't call me, I'll call you' thing. And with that dream still affecting her it would be hard to act normal.

The bedroom door was open so she strolled out naked and straight to the living area. At least there she had a basket of clean clothes that she hadn't put away yet. She picked up a pair of panties then slipped them on before grabbing a T-shirt and pulling it over her head. Once she was covered she walked over to the large windows and yanked open the curtains. She had a beautiful view of the Pacific Ocean and she enjoyed seeing it when the sun was just rising over the water.

Even though she'd lived there for a few years now she wasn't used to seeing all the openness. The Pack that she'd grown up in had been located in the middle of the woods. She'd given up the freedom of nature to surround herself with water and city people.

Marissa pressed her hand against the cool pane of glass and closed her eyes. Why did she have to dream about things that she would never have? It was impossible for her to ever have her fantasies become reality. She was alone and she should be used to that, but Marissa craved the intimate touch of someone who would accept her. Even if she was broken. She'd been on her own for so long now that she figured the feelings of loneliness would have disappeared. Instead the feeling was stronger than ever.

But she was a grown woman and didn't have time to let her despair rise. She pushed off the window and turned to go into the kitchen. It was only a dream and she would forget about that and the male wolf that didn't exist. At least not for her. The coffee pot was ready to go so all she had to do was press the power button. After she got some caffeine inside her she could get rid of her guest.

If I could only remember his name.

Damn, she hated when the full moon was close. It was the only time she didn't have complete control over her shifter side. Marissa might be defective but she did get horny around this time of month like so many of the other shifters. She didn't know if it was a wolf thing or what. It wasn't like she could ask anyone either. Her family was gone except for her sister, Elizabeth. And Marissa would not be asking her sister about her sex life. Elizabeth was much more conservative than she was.

The beep from the machine let her know that her coffee was ready. She strolled back over to the counter then reached up and pulled down a mug. Marissa poured some of the dark brew into the cup before adding some sugar. She stirred it slowly as she breathed in the fragrant aroma. If there was anything that she spent too much money on it was her organic and expensive coffee—a habit she had picked up when she'd first moved into the small coastal town. She lifted the mug to her lips and blew on the liquid inside, then took a sip.

"Ah," she murmured in happiness.

"That smells great. Can I get a cup?"

She jerked slightly, not having heard her companion wake and walk around her condo. She turned and smiled at him. Damn, he was built. He had long black hair with beautiful blue eyes. His chest, arms and back were muscular and he had a hard six-pack. Yeah, she'd picked damn well the night before. She licked her lips as he stood there in just a pair of jeans, still unbuttoned, and looking sexy as hell.

Chad, she could remember his name now. They'd met at the local bar that she liked to visit because it had rough, biker-type patrons. For a human he sure had given her one hell of a ride.

"Sure." She waved him forward. "Come on in."

He grinned, showing perfectly straight white teeth.

Hmm, maybe she could take him back to bed for an encore. If the dream could help with anything maybe it would get her into the right mood. Chad was nothing like the wolf in her dream. Of course, he was human, but he also couldn't force her to submit the way that only a strong shifter male could. Still, it would be a waste to send him away while she was tingling with need. She'd make his drink and let things grow from there.

"How do you take your coffee?" she asked.

"Black is fine," he replied against her ear as he stepped up behind her.

She shivered slightly from the huskiness of his voice. Marissa grabbed another mug then filled it up before she turned to face him.

The look in his eye was telling her he wouldn't mind another round either. She handed him the cup, making sure to let her fingers brush his. He accepted it with his right hand but wrapped his left around her back. He pulled her close as he dipped his head.

"I really enjoyed last night," he said.

"Me too," she agreed. Marissa ran her hand over his naked chest. "You sure know how to show a girl a good time."

He chuckled. "It's easy when I'm with the right partner."

Marissa flushed. Yeah, she had been up for anything with the full moon just a day away. Chad nuzzled her neck then gave her a quick nip. The move was so unexpected that she jumped. It was almost wolf-like. She knew he was human but that small sting was perfect. A repeat was very much needed indeed. He set his mug down on the countertop with a loud clunk before he gripped her hips, lifting her up.

As she landed on the marble top he stepped between her legs. Marissa was glad she hadn't gotten completely dressed. She ran her hand over the muscles on his chest then bent forward and licked one of his nipples. He groaned while threading his fingers through her hair. Marissa scooted closer to the edge so she could get a better angle. While tracing her tongue from one pec to the other, she trailed her hands down his stomach toward the waistband of his jeans.

"Yeah," he murmured and rocked his hips as she slid her hands into the denim.

He was fully erect and she wanted to get a taste.

A loud banging on her front door stopped her from dropping into position.

Chad groaned but helped her slide off the counter. She offered him a smile then patted his chest before she headed toward the door. A glance at the clock in the living room showed her that it was just after nine in the morning. Marissa had no idea who would be at her place so early on a Saturday morning. What if she wanted to sleep in? That was just rude.

When she reached the front door she looked out of the peephole to see who was there. A young man in a brown shirt and shorts stood shuffling his feet while holding an envelope. She wasn't expecting a delivery but unlocked and opened the door anyway. Maybe the kid had the wrong address.

"Yes?" she asked.

"Marissa Boyd?" the young man asked.

"Yes."

"I have an overnight letter for you," he said.

"From who?" Why would anyone send a letter through a service that would cost so much?

The kid glanced down at the notepad in his other hand. "It's from an Elizabeth Boyd in Texas."

Her sister. Now Marissa was really curious. "Okay," she said, reaching out for the envelope.

"I need you to sign this, please." He offered her the clipboard with a pen attached by a string.

Marissa smiled as she signed her name quickly then handed it back. The young man passed her the envelope. It was pretty light so it didn't seem to have anything big in it. "Thanks," she murmured but wasn't really paying the delivery kid any more attention. She closed the door and shook the package.

"Everything okay?" Chad asked from the kitchen

doorway.

"Hmm," she responded distractedly, starting to tear open the package. She shook out a smaller envelope. The paper was made from high quality stock with her name and address written beautifully. She would know her sister's writing anywhere.

Marissa dropped the envelope onto the coffee table as she walked toward the window. She thought she heard Chad say something but she didn't respond. Instead, she shuffled the letter from one hand to the other. Until she opened it she could ignore whatever Elizabeth had to say. Good or bad. Not that she didn't love her sister, but no news was usually the best news. Elizabeth currently lived with a Pack and she was happy so there was no reason for her to write a letter when she could just call. They tried to speak on the phone every few weeks but never saw each other anymore. Marissa refused to visit and Elizabeth had a good job and a boyfriend, not allowing her to find the time to come to California.

"Here we go," Marissa muttered then tore open the back of the envelope. She pulled out the heavy card and flipped it over.

We cordially invite you...

Marissa stared at the printed words. She was doing it — finally, Elizabeth was taking a mate. When Elizabeth had moved to Texas it was because she'd met Greg. Greg was also a teacher and they both worked at a local elementary school and had been dating for several years. Marissa had known that this day would come, but she still had several emotions running through her.

She was jealous and that wasn't fair to her sister. Marissa was also happy for Elizabeth and hoped she would be able to show that.

In the ten years that they'd been separated from each other, Marissa had encouraged Elizabeth to follow her dreams, whether with her career or when she'd met Greg. Elizabeth needed to go for what she wanted, and it seemed she was finally *getting* what she wanted.

Just because Marissa would never have the life she craved didn't mean that she wanted Elizabeth to suffer any longer. For as long as she could remember, Elizabeth was always paying for Marissa's sins. Luckily Elizabeth had gotten away from the Pack they had been born into. Once Marissa had left, it'd opened the door to Elizabeth being accepted into another Pack.

Inside the invitation was a folded up piece of paper. Marissa opened it to find a handwritten note.

Marissa,

I know this won't be easy for you but I need you here with me to celebrate the ceremony. I won't do this without you. I know I'm asking a lot but I hope you can spend a few days with me to help me prepare and be with me when I say my vows to Greg. Don't say no. Please come.

With all my love,

Elizabeth

Well shit, how could she say no to the only thing Elizabeth had ever asked for?

"You okay?"

She jumped when Chad joined her by the window. Marissa dropped her hands but didn't let go of the letter or the invitation.

Chad nodded to her hands. "Bad news?" He'd dressed and had even put on his shoes. She guessed this was the end of their fun. Oh well, she really wasn't in the mood any longer and she had some thinking to do. Instead of answering him she only shrugged.

"I'm sorry," he said.

Then he surprised her by leaning forward and kissing her forehead. She wasn't used to such an intimate gesture. She closed her eyes for a moment to hold in the warm feeling.

"Thanks," she whispered.

"I would like to see you again," he said. "I left my number on your counter. I hope you'll call me."

She nodded, really not sure how else to respond. Maybe

it wouldn't be too bad to date a human. She stayed away from relationships because she craved a shifter but had to settle for a human. It was better to just have one-night stands than not be able to give her partner one hundred percent of herself. Or that was what she'd always believed. Perhaps she needed to change her way of thinking. At least she wouldn't be alone anymore.

"Take care of yourself," he told her. "And call me."

Marissa watched as he walked away. Damn, the man really did have a nice ass. Too bad they'd gotten interrupted. With a sigh she turned back to the window. Using her heightened sight she could see the waves crashing against the sand on the shore. It was peaceful but her thoughts weren't. She had to start making plans to go to Texas next month.

Fucking Texas.

Chapter One

Marissa took a drink of the coffee she'd picked up at the last gas station. The hot liquid burned her tongue and tasted like sludge. It wasn't Starbucks, that was for sure, but she didn't expect any different in the middle of fucking nowhere. She had flown into Texas International Airport and rented a car to drive the rest of the way to the small town her sister called home. And small town was giving the place a lot of credit. The entire area between El Paso and the Panhandle was made up of tiny towns that even if they were combined wouldn't be as big as Dallas. There wasn't even a mall for at least another three hours. Not that she wanted to go shopping but it would be nice to have options. It was still a shock to her how excited her sister Elizabeth had been about moving here, but looking at the passing scenery of trees, trees and more trees, Marissa didn't get it. What could anyone like about the middle of nowhere? No buildings, other cars, or people around.

Rolling her window down and turning Bon Jovi even louder on the stereo, she concentrated on the drive—not the reason for coming. She dreaded going into Pack territory, but Elizabeth was the only family she had left, and, after finding her mate, Elizabeth wanted Marissa there for the mating ceremony.

That thought brought a smile to Marissa's face as she glanced at the invitation on the seat next to her. She wanted Elizabeth to be happy, and Greg sounded like a nice guy. She'd spoken to him numerous times on the phone, and he'd always been respectful toward her. And that wasn't common. A were who couldn't shift was an outsider. And everyone except Elizabeth had treated her that way her entire life.

Marissa had left the Pack she'd been raised in as soon as she could. Never to set foot in any Pack territory again. That was until later today. Elizabeth, on the other hand, had stayed until she'd met Greg, a member of a different Pack. They had met during one of the few conferences Elizabeth had attended. After the initial meeting, Greg's Pack had offered her a teaching position at the elementary school and she had taken it. He had been courting her ever since with the blessing of her new Pack Alpha, Gage Wolf.

Seriously, Elizabeth's Alpha's last name was Wolf. *Could he have not come up with anything better? Maybe tried to hide what he was?* Marissa just knew that Gage was going to be an arrogant, cocky, infuriating man. She was not looking forward to meeting him. Greg, however, she was actually excited to get to know.

Marissa chuckled, thinking of everything Greg had done to win her sister's heart. He'd known he'd wanted Elizabeth and had patiently waited. It had taken Elizabeth a year to agree to the mating ceremony, but she finally had. Marissa knew one of the reasons Elizabeth had been holding off was because of her. Elizabeth was a good person, and, even though Marissa had told her numerous times that Elizabeth needed to live her life as a full shifter, the guilt still hit Elizabeth.

Sometimes Marissa thought her non-shifter status was harder on her sister than herself. Marissa wasn't good enough to belong to a Pack but Elizabeth still tried to get her interested in that kind of life. It had added stress between the two of them until Marissa avoided Elizabeth's calls most of the time. That was probably why Elizabeth had gone the route of private messenger.

She hadn't meant to let so much time to go by without talking to her sister and Marissa always intended to return her messages, but life seemed to get in the way.

It didn't help that Elizabeth really didn't understand how

Marissa felt about things.

Marissa had the same instincts as any other were and with that came the need for a Pack, but she had given up on that a long time ago. She'd grown up alone and would always remain that way—in the middle, between a shifter and a human. She had many gifts due to her genes—the extended lifespan, the wolf traits and some enhanced features—but not enough. Elizabeth thought Marissa could belong with her. Elizabeth was wrong and Marissa really hoped that she would concentrate on her ceremony and not nag her.

Marissa would put everything she had into this week and the ceremony that meant so much to her only sibling. Even if she would rather have been anywhere else. But she did love Elizabeth, she looked up to her sister, and had to push down the bit of jealousy that she always felt.

The differences between her and Elizabeth had grown as they had aged. That was why Marissa had never visited Elizabeth's new home. She wasn't scared of being in Pack territory, she just didn't want to face all the males and their egos. And from what she understood, the Pack's Alpha or leader, was pretty young himself.

When around other wolves, the female wolf inside her demanded that she mate with one of her own kind. So, as long as she avoided everyone except her sister as much as she could and kept her urges inside, everything would be okay. She would not act like the wolf she couldn't shift into.

And if the Alpha was anything like her old one, she'd just tell him where to stick it. The idea of telling the Alpha of a territory to go to hell made her smile wider and laugh harder. She wasn't seventeen anymore. She wasn't a scared little girl who had to follow everything someone told her. No, she was a grown woman. And she was going to enjoy the time with her sister.

She wasn't dressed to impress the Alpha or any men in the territory as she currently wore a pair of hip-hugging jeans and a tight pink T-shirt. The paint on her toenails matched the color of her shirt, as did the flip-flops. It was a far cry from the suit she wore every day as an office assistant. She felt free.

As much as she avoided being around shifter territory, her wolf craved the chance to run free. She would be on two legs instead of four but, after months inside the bustling crowded streets in a city, Marissa hoped to get a couple of private moments in the woods.

When she almost missed the turn-off to the territory gate, she jerked the wheel sharply to the left. The back of the car skidded around and kicked up dirt. Laughing, she straightened the car and slowed her speed. She didn't think Gage Wolf would be happy if she took out a couple of trees.

Why did this Pack located in the middle of nowhere need a fence and a guard station?

She reached the gate and rolled to a stop to wait for the guard. He didn't disappoint. A man over six feet came over to the window then leaned down, smiling at her.

"Can I help you?" he asked in a husky voice.

She took a deep breath and smiled back. If all the men were this good-looking, she would have her work cut out for her trying to keep her distance. They'd flirt and tease with her, and she'd have to be strong and resist, because as soon as they knew her secret, she wouldn't exist any longer to them. And no matter what she said to herself, the rejection always hurt.

"I'm Elizabeth Boyd's sister. I need directions to her house, please."

His smile didn't change and he nodded. "Give me just a minute." He winked then headed to the guard house and picked up the phone.

Marissa watched his ass flex under the tight pair of jeans he was wearing. At least as he made his call she got to enjoy the view.

The guard glanced over his shoulder at her and she waved. Yeah, she was still here and wasn't going anywhere. He was no doubt checking with the Alpha to make sure she could come in and play. With her own sister, no less,

Marissa thought bitterly.

She kept her face friendly and her thoughts to herself as he came back to the car. "Problem?"

"Not at all," he said, shaking his head, and gave her directions to her sister's house. "My name's Steve if you want to get together later," he added.

Not in this life.

"Hmm, we'll see." She was careful not to commit to anything he could hold her to later. The laws of the Pack were much different from the laws where she lived. Marissa knew them all and had only ever broken one.

Shaking that unpleasant thought from her head, she drove through the gate. Looking back into the rear-view mirror, she saw Steve standing with a smile on his face.

"Down, girl," she told herself. "This is Pack territory."

The gravel crunched under her tires as Marissa made sure to keep her speed slow. She wasn't going to give anyone any reason to mess with her.

The grounds of the territory were absolutely beautiful. Thick, dark green grass went on as far as she could see. Behind a row of houses, tall and healthy trees rose up toward the sky. At least the property was pretty. Maybe she would enjoy herself just a little.

* * * *

Gage Wolf hung up the phone in his study and glanced at the clock. Elizabeth's sister had made good time. When Elizabeth had told him she wanted her sister here for the ceremony, he'd thought it was a good idea. He'd still not met the young woman but he'd asked about Elizabeth and her entire family when Greg had first brought up the option of Elizabeth joining the Pack.

He remembered the conversations he'd had with Elizabeth about her sister when he was first considering accepting Elizabeth into his Pack.

Elizabeth was protective and worried about her younger

sibling. He understood it must have been hard for a non-shifter to grow up, but he didn't get why Marissa refused to see her sister.

And that, he knew, was the main reason Elizabeth had held back on the ceremony for so long. Gage was determined not to allow Marissa to hold Elizabeth back from what she wanted. And she wanted Greg.

At the knock on his door, he looked up. His second-in-command, Logan, poked his head in. "I'm taking off now."

Gage nodded.

"Want to go for a run later?" Logan asked as he opened the door wider to lean against the jamb.

"I'll be going by the Boyd house tonight," Gage told him, watching his friend and Pack member smile.

"I don't think you'll be the only one."

"What do you mean?"

The mischievous twinkle in his eyes was unmistakable. "Steve might have mentioned to a few of the guys how hot she is."

Gage shook his head. Steve hadn't wasted any time if Logan already knew. Gage didn't need further complications. "She's not here to mate."

Logan laughed. "Well, that may be beside the point."

"She doesn't need to be bothered."

"Well, who is to say it would bother her? She is a were."

"Yes, but still..." Gage wasn't sure why he already felt protective toward her. His best guess would be that Elizabeth had shared the secret of her sister not being able to shift and how it still affected her. While it wouldn't be a problem to his Pack members, he didn't want the girl overwhelmed with attention. Like most men, male shifters loved the chase of attracting a mate. They could just be more direct in their pursuit.

"Well, then you might want to get over there." With that, Logan turned and left.

Cursing, Gage stood then followed his friend down the hall. Gage cut through the living room to exit from the sliding door in the study. As the cool night air hit him, he rolled his neck and shoulders. A run would have probably been a good idea. It had only been a couple of days but he loved to shift into his other form. It gave him the freedom that he didn't get in his normal day-to-day life. All day long he was answering questions while at the same time his shifters had everything they needed. It was nice to let the wolf reign for a while. Not that he wasn't fully aware of what he was doing or his surroundings when in his shifted form. He just couldn't answer questions without the ability to speak.

Gage hurried down the curved path that would take him from the Alpha house to some of the other homes. He needed to set the ground rules down for his Pack toward this woman but first he needed to warn Marissa of the chance of having quite a few men at her tail. He hoped in the time she'd been away from her Pack and on her own that she'd found contentment. Gage worried about any ill effects from this stranger being in his territory on Elizabeth. Greg and Elizabeth deserved happiness.

Gage walked up to Elizabeth's attractive two-story house a few minutes later. Before he could ring the bell, the door opened and a young Pack member walked out onto the porch.

Gage stepped aside to let the man pass. Jeff looked surprised to see him before quickly dropping his eyes.

"Alpha."

Gage nodded his hello and strolled through the open doorway and right into the middle of a conversation in progress.

"I'm going upstairs to unpack. If you have any more visitors, tell them to come back in a week. I can't believe they all need to come by right now to congratulate you on your mating ceremony."

"That's not what this is about and you know it," Elizabeth said calmly.

"Well, I'm not a circus freak show!"

He hadn't gotten a good view of Marissa but he'd clearly heard her frustration. They really should have figured this would happen and done their best to prevent her being bombarded by eligible men.

Elizabeth stood with her back to him, her hands clasped tightly behind her, and sighed. She stiffened and he knew he'd been scented. She turned and faced Gage with a surprised look on her face.

"Gage," she greeted.

He wasn't certain if it was in welcome or not. He could practically feel the tension coming off her.

"I didn't know you were coming by. I mean, I thought you might, but with so many..." She looked nervously around her.

He only lifted an eyebrow. "I take it you've had a lot of guests?"

Elizabeth didn't appear amused. "Yeah, and it's driving her crazy. I'm sorry. I don't know where my manners are. Please come in."

Gage entered the living room, immediately taking in the new scent and the others mixed in with it. He could have named the wolves that had stopped by. There was only one smell he didn't recognize, and that had to be Elizabeth's sister.

His nostrils flared as he inhaled the fresh wood and spice smell that had his body immediately coming to life. He knew that if her scent was so alluring he was going to have his hands full keeping the available wolves away from her.

"I'll go get Marissa."

Gage laid a gentle hand on her arm. "I'll go up. I need to talk to her privately."

Elizabeth seemed uncertain for a moment, shifting on her feet and glancing upstairs.

"I just want to welcome her, tell her a few things about the ceremony, and make sure she understands some Pack rules."

Elizabeth nodded. He was sure she was worried about

not only her sister but him also. Greg had mentioned the amount of stress that had been mounting.

"She… She's not always the nicest."

Elizabeth looked away when she said it, and Gage knew it wasn't easy for her to be in between her sister and her Alpha.

Gage smiled and patted her arm. "Don't worry. We'll both be fine," Gage assured her.

That seemed to console Elizabeth, and she nodded. "I'll just be in the kitchen starting dinner then."

Gage listened as he made his way upstairs. He could hear Marissa muttering to herself from down the hall.

He walked into the bedroom and stopped in his tracks. It was one of the most amazing sights he'd ever seen—her butt was sticking out from under the bed with her legs tucked under her. She moved from side to side and Gage felt himself growing hard.

He growled at the reaction, and she must have heard because there was a bang against the bottom of the bed, followed by another stream of curses.

She peered from under the bed, then crawled out, rubbing her head.

"What the hell are you doing in here?" she demanded.

"I was going to ask you the same thing. Do you always crawl under beds?"

Marissa gave him the once-over. Her attraction was immediate—he sensed it. Gage heard her heartbeat pick up and watched while she wiped her hands nervously on her pants. She shifted from foot to foot and he smelled her arousal. The stubborn look on her face told him she was going to fight it.

"Gage Wolf?"

Even though he was certain she knew exactly who he was, she'd phrased it as a question.

Gage nodded at the beauty in front of him. To say he was taken by surprise was an understatement. Where Elizabeth was pale and slender with blue eyes and blonde hair, her sister looked nothing like her.

She had long dark hair and crystal green eyes that were narrowed. It was quite obvious she didn't like her attraction to him, but he couldn't say the same. It had been a very long time since he'd felt this instant hunger.

"I am," he answered her unnecessary question. "And you are Marissa."

Marissa nodded, trying to swallow past the lump in her throat. His voice was deep and she could almost feel it wrapping around her. This reaction wasn't good and she needed to get herself under control.

He was absolutely, positively the best-looking man she had ever seen. He was taller than she was—she'd guess over six-two. He wore black slacks and a button-down shirt with the sleeves rolled up.

"Is there something you needed?" she asked, crossing her arms over her chest, feeling defensive. She was too skinny, her hair was a mess, and she was tired.

Gage followed the gesture with his eyes, and Marissa blushed when she realized she had just brought more attention to herself.

"I came to welcome you to my territory as is proper for any Pack Alpha," Gage said, taking a step closer. "And to go over some rules."

Marissa stiffened at his words, although unsurprised by them. She could guess what rules he was going to make sure she knew. She'd heard them all her life.

"You were raised in a Pack?" he asked.

Marissa nodded a second time, though he was asking a question he already had the answer to. Elizabeth had already told her that Gage was aware of her secret. Marissa had not been happy with her sister but she could understand why Elizabeth had felt it necessary to tell him.

"I don't expect things will be much different here," he said.

Marissa didn't either. "I understand," she said, stiffening

her shoulders and fisting her hands at her side.

"Do you have any questions for me?"

The pep talk she had given herself on the drive allowed her to speak calmly. "No, I don't believe I have any questions about my behavior here. I assure you that I have no interest in your Pack. One week — seven days — I'll be here. I think you can deal with it as I have to. Then I'll be gone and you won't have to worry about me corrupting your precious Pack."

When she finished, something like surprise crossed his face briefly, and he growled. No one had probably ever spoken to him that way before. But Marissa wasn't going to be intimidated.

When he took a step closer, she could sense the anger and confusion from him.

"I'll warn you once about the way you talk to me. I don't know how your Alpha reacted, but that kind of disrespect will not be tolerated here."

Marissa didn't tell him that she'd never been brave enough to talk to her old Alpha like that. Marissa backed up as the Alpha stepped closer.

"Also, I know how long you are here for. I know a selfish woman like you wouldn't give up more than a week for the sister who loves her. Someone who has waited far too long to be happy because of you."

His words stopped her retreat. "Selfish? You just called me selfish."

Even with the smile that touched his lips, he didn't look any less furious. "I did."

"Well, let me tell you something, Mr. Wolf. I wouldn't be here if I didn't love my sister. I wouldn't set foot in this territory if it had not meant so much to Elizabeth. I gave my blessing to her a long time ago." Marissa took a deep breath as she wound down. She realized she was explaining herself to him and, not wanting to give him any information he could use on her later, she quickly tried to cover her outburst. "Not that it's any of your business."

Marissa backed up until she touched the wall and Gage closed the distance between them.

"You do know who I am. My status here?"

Marissa didn't trust the smooth smile or easy tone. "Yes."

"So are you trying to piss me off? Any intelligent person would know better than to tell an Alpha a Pack member wasn't his business or make the comments you have." When he reached forward and grabbed her arm, it was too fast for Marissa to avoid. "I feel sorry for the troubles you must have given to your Pack leader."

The electricity that flowed through Marissa's body at Gage's touch drew a startled breath from her. He must have felt it too, because he immediately let go of her. Marissa stared at him as neither spoke for several minutes. She grasped at anything she could say to make him go away.

"I don't have a Pack leader. But I do know how to address the Alpha of a Pack who has been kind enough to let me visit. I apologize. My attitude and disrespectful comments were uncalled for." Fear and uncertainty had her lowering her eyes to the floor in a submissive gesture. It galled her to show any submission to him, but his touch unnerved her.

She could feel his stare even though she wasn't looking at him and barely stopped herself from shuffling her feet. The urge to run coursed strongly through her body.

"I accept your apology," Gage said quietly. "I might not know everything you've been through but I do understand that you haven't always felt welcome with our kind. I expect you to tell me if you have any problems. I'll get the Pack to give you some space but you will have to interact with them."

When he'd finally spoken, she'd been so surprised that she'd lifted her eyes to meet his. Why would he even want her to talk to them? She was confused and it was really hard to concentrate, having him so close.

For a brief moment she regretted what she was. A shifter unable to change, an abomination, someone who should have been drowned at birth. She'd come to terms with it a long time ago but Gage was making her wonder what could have been if she'd been normal.

This was why she hung around with humans. They couldn't hurt her with their words and the fact that none of them would truly accept her.

"I'll be on my best behavior," she said softly. Maybe she wasn't as badass as she pretended but no one other than herself and Gage would have to know that.

"Very well then. Now, I believe your sister is downstairs about to have a fit with us up here arguing, so I suggest we finish this another time."

Marissa dipped her head in acknowledgment, relieved that he would leave now. Maybe he was just as unsettled as she was.

Gage walked out without another word to her. Marissa sat on her bed and thought about what had just taken place. She looked up at a sound in the hall and saw Elizabeth standing at the entrance to her guest room with wide eyes and a frown.

"Don't start," Marissa warned.

Elizabeth shook her head. "Gage is a nice man and a good Alpha."

Marissa smiled even though she felt her face wanting to crack. "I'm sure he is," she lied.

Chapter Two

Gage wasn't surprised at the knock on his office door, though it did annoy him. Logan opened the door and walked in without hesitation. He grinned at Gage as he sat and lounged on the couch.

"What?" Gage asked, not in the mood for any more games tonight.

"Sam said he ran into you after you met with the Boyd woman." Logan paused for dramatic effect. It was something Gage usually found amusing. Tonight wasn't one of those times. "He said you seemed agitated."

Gage snorted in response. "I am not agitated."

Logan nodded, his expression growing serious. "No, I didn't think so. If you were agitated, you might be pacing your office liked a caged...wolf."

Gage didn't miss the twitch in Logan's lips. His second in command kept the smile from his face this time, but barely. "I am not pacing."

"No. Absolutely no pacing going on here," Logan agreed too easily, proving that he was finding too much humor in messing with his Alpha.

"I have had enough with foolish talk for one night, so knock it off." Gage barely kept the growl out of his voice.

Logan's blue eyes sparkled. "Things didn't go so well with Elizabeth's sister, I take it?"

Gage snorted again and went back to pacing. "She's rude, stubborn, and..."

"Beautiful?"

Gage swirled around. "How do you know she's beautiful?"

To Logan's credit, he kept a straight face giving only a careless shrug. "A lot of the men were quite impressed with her."

"She is not here to be hit on by every available male in the territory," he said strongly. Too strongly even to his own ears.

"Well, since she was raised in a Pack, I don't think this behavior is that new to her," Logan predicted. No doubt trying to be helpful.

Gage didn't respond.

"Being raised in a Pack, she already knows most rules and our laws," Logan continued.

"Oh, she knows the rules all right. Knows how to ignore them."

Logan nodded as if he understood. "It's not the first time you have encountered a rogue or undisciplined wolf. What makes her different?"

That question was what was bothering Gage. "I don't know what caused it. There's more to her story than just leaving her Pack because she didn't feel comfortable not being able to shift. Or a break-up. There's a pain deep inside her and I want to know where it comes from."

"She's only going to be here a week," Logan pointed out.

"Yes but in that time she'll be protected. I think that's what she needs. There is no one out there making sure she's safe and cared for. I wouldn't be a good Alpha if I didn't help in any way I can."

"As long as that's all this is," Logan said.

"What's that supposed to mean?" Gage demanded. He narrowed his eyes, ensuring Logan knew he was serious. They didn't get into many power battles but every now and then Logan challenged Gage. Not for Alpha status but in a way that Gage knew his friend was concerned.

"I don't want you to get hurt," Logan said. "She's not going to stay."

"Just get me everything you can on her."

Logan stood then left Gage once again alone in his office.

"Let's see what secrets you have, Marissa Boyd," he said quietly. He turned back to his desk where he'd left his laptop. He would do some research of his own.

* * * *

After dinner, Marissa claimed to be tired from her trip and locked herself in her room. She was exhausted but really needed some time alone. Elizabeth's future mate had joined them for dinner and Marissa had to admit she liked Greg even more than she'd thought she would.

It was obvious that he only had eyes for Elizabeth. Marissa didn't miss the subtle touches that passed between the two of them either. Marissa was thrilled for her sister, but there was just a hint of jealousy deep down. She tried to push it away, but it was there—just as it had always been. Along with the question that haunted her late at night. Why was it that Marissa was defective?

Deciding a bath would soothe her, Marissa filled the tub with hot water then relaxed into the marble enclosure. Her sister's house was nice. It was very homey and wasn't too fancy. It was so different from the huge, cold house they'd grown up in. She thought this home matched Elizabeth just as this territory seemed to.

Marissa sighed, thinking about the territory. She had been shocked when Alpha Gage hadn't demanded she leave. She had been rude to him. She didn't know of any other Alpha who wouldn't have punished her. And he would have had every right. She was his guest and was expected to follow his rules. It might have been more complicated if she had a Pack Alpha standing for her, but she had no one. She didn't have anyone in her corner to help her smooth things over with him. It was Marissa's responsibility to make sure she didn't cause any problems. If only she'd come in later in the week instead of for the entire seven days.

She'd missed Elizabeth, though, so she'd packed her bag and purchased a plane ticket. She really needed to work on not being so rash. She had no idea how she was going to make it through seven days around the Alpha. Thinking about Gage had her temperature rising. Oh, he was a good-looking man, although there was more to him than just that. There was power there—that was unmistakable—but she sensed something different in him from her old Alpha. Even though they had argued, she didn't have the same fear of his power as she did others in his position. Oh, she had been scared, but if Gage had continued to touch her she was more worried about her own reaction. She'd wanted him, an Alpha. It was like she could feel the compassion inside him for others. That could only lead to trouble.

She'd given her heart once to a wolf, and it had ended badly. Very badly, and he hadn't been an Alpha. She wouldn't repeat that mistake. Although the Alpha was tempting. So very tempting that Marissa found herself caressing her breasts thinking about him.

This wasn't a normal reaction for her. She could always resist her urges. The wolf inside her might not like it, but she could do it. Her only fear was that Gage could push past her defenses and make her vulnerable.

She dipped a hand under the water and rubbed the ache between her legs. She made a vow to herself right then and there. She would never be vulnerable again. Even if it left her sexually frustrated.

She let her fingers trail over the swollen folds of her sex before slipping inside. The pressure of two fingers entering felt so good. With her other hand, she pulled and pinched her nipple. The slight pain added to her arousal.

Marissa closed her eyes, and it was Gage's face that popped into her head. What would he do if he walked in and saw her touching herself?

Weres were very sexual, and Marissa had stronger urges than most women she knew. She indulged herself often but only with humans who couldn't hurt her. Even the man she'd been with the night she'd received Elizabeth's invitation hadn't evoked an ounce of fear. Sure, he'd been big and strong but he was still human. She tried to picture his face as she played with her pussy but her mind kept returning to the Alpha. Gage Wolf. She shuddered. His presence was so dominating that she could almost *feel* his eyes on her.

Would Gage drop to his knees beside her? Place his hand with hers? Pump his thick fingers inside her?

Marissa let out a low, long moan at the thought. Her fingers moved easily between the folds of her core, building the release she needed. She wondered what he looked like without his clothes. His tan arms had been revealed earlier. Even with his clothes, she could tell he was built. She'd bet he had a wonderful body.

Fingers moving faster, Marissa lifted her hips as she finally reached her climax. Biting her lip, she came slowly but fully with thoughts of Gage teasing her.

* * * *

Gage stared at the information in front of him. "They just let her go?" he asked, looking over to Logan.

The other man glanced up from the pages he was reading. "Apparently."

Gage shook his head. "Something's wrong here. They didn't even try to keep track of her." He could picture a young Marissa alone and scared, out of the Pack for the first time. His anger rose and it was all he could do to keep control of his wolf.

Logan placed the papers on the sofa next to him. "This is not telling us anything. It leads to more questions than answers. You need to talk to this girl again."

Gage nodded, looking past Logan to the window in his office. Thoughts of Marissa Boyd had kept him up last night. The full moon was only six nights away, and every wolf got distracted as it came closer, but he was more than just *distracted* by this woman. If the hard-on he was sporting was any indication, he needed to do more with her than just talk. It'd been years since he'd felt this hot for any woman.

"Alpha?"

Snapping his head up, he didn't miss the amusement all over Logan's face. "I'll go talk to her."

"Elizabeth should still be teaching, so you should have all morning alone...so you can talk privately."

Gage barely contained his groan. Not only had he been hard since first seeing this woman, but it seemed his Beta was determined to get him together with her.

"I'm just going over to talk to her." Gage stood, stretching his back from sitting too long at his desk. He wasn't even saying the words to Logan. He was reminding himself. Marissa was nervous and jumpy around him and he didn't want her to feel pressured. But if she gave him even the smallest hint that she wanted him as much, Gage would pounce. He wasn't going to torture himself if Marissa shared the attraction. And he knew she already did from their first meeting. He just wanted her to have to admit it. "I won't be gone too long."

"Of course, Alpha," Logan agreed, not bothering to hide his huge grin as he left Gage's office.

Maybe Gage would come back to the house and take Logan down a few notches. That wouldn't take care of the most pressing problem but it might make him feel better. If Gage was going to be sexually frustrated, a fight would at least take some of his own edginess away.

He had a feeling that any amount of time spent with Marissa was going to test his control.

Marissa stood on her sister's back porch, looking out at the woods that surrounded the house. It was so beautiful here. The warm wind blew her bangs into her face and she brushed her hair away. The quietness of the area was soothing, and being alone, getting to bask in nature, almost brought tears of happiness to her eyes. How long had it been since she'd just opened up to this feeling?

She remembered a time when she'd hated having to be

around crowds. In the years since she'd left her Pack, she had gotten used to people and the noise. What she had once hated now served the purpose of keeping her from having to admit that she'd never have what her sister did. This place was too beautiful for the likes of Marissa. She had to pay penance for her past mistakes. Giving up a view like this was her punishment. Elizabeth didn't understand but Marissa didn't expect her sister to either.

They used to stay up late talking in the room they shared, about the perfect place to make a home. This territory was everything they'd wanted growing up and Elizabeth had finally found it. Marissa had to push down the kernel of resentment that wanted to grow. No, Elizabeth belonged and she didn't. Even if the property was picture perfect and, what she'd dreamed about. Foolish wishes of a teen who hadn't understood how the world really worked.

Back then, Marissa had still had hope that one day the Pack would accept her. She no longer carried that hope. It had been replaced by the bitterness that she didn't belong anywhere. The wind called for her wolf to run. She couldn't. She literally could not shift.

The thick green grass cushioned her bare feet as she stepped onto it. The animal inside moved restlessly to be let out. Her skin prickled and she shivered. The wolf needed to be released. Normally she would do this with sex, but this was not the place for her to indulge. It was going to be a painful and agonizing week.

Moving farther away from the porch toward the edge of the trees, Marissa felt her wolf jump inside her skin. Some weres thought of their animal as an extension of themselves. Marissa was different. From an early age she'd determined that her wolf was separate. A part of her that was suppressed so hard that the animal and human were not linked. Since no one knew why she couldn't transform like other shifters, Marissa figured her feelings were just as good as what anyone else thought.

She scratched her arms out of habit because of the feelings

she was having. God, how she wished she could shift. Could let the wolf completely free like it wanted, like it needed.

But that wasn't going to happen. Resigned and unhappy, she turned back toward the house and stopped short, noticing the man who stood on the porch watching her. Her wolf growled its approval, demanding she take this available male.

Marissa tried to push the feeling aside but if she couldn't run like a wolf she wanted to have sex. It didn't help that she couldn't stop thinking about the hot Alpha.

Gage watched as Marissa's eyes widened. She licked her lips, and his cock jumped in his jeans. He'd been surprised to find her staring into the woods like she was ready to go running. He didn't know much about non-shifters. They were not common. Only a handful of them existed. But the intensity of her stare was like that before a shift.

He quickly covered the distance between them. Marissa didn't move away from him when he reached her. Her green eyes had started to glow.

"The wild calls to you?"

She nodded and licked her lips again.

"How does it make you feel? Not being able to shift?" He wanted to know more about her. He wanted to reach the woman, and the wolf, under the skin. Maybe if she felt he understood her she'd open up to him.

She looked so sad he wanted to wrap his arms around her and tell her everything would be okay. He couldn't make that promise to her, though, at least not yet. Hopefully soon he'd be able to guarantee her safety and acceptance.

She cleared her throat twice before speaking. "Trapped."

Her words broke his heart a little. She had started shaking so he reached for her and pulled her into his arms for comfort. "Does it hurt?" He couldn't imagine how it would feel for his wolf to be trapped.

When she only shrugged a shoulder, he continued, "What can I do?"

Her gaze met his before dropping to his lips. Fuck, his cock was hard and he wanted to plunder her mouth. The moment she sucked her bottom lip, the last thread of his resolve slipped. He yanked her to him before taking control of her mouth. She didn't fight him, but opened immediately. He plunged his tongue inside, dominating the kiss. Her low moan only drove him on farther, harder. With one hand wrapped in her hair, holding her head still, he used the other to bring their bodies closer.

Her lips moved under his while she clawed at the shirt on his back. Knowing she was as out of control as he was feeling was amazing. It seemed there was much more to this woman than he had thought. He didn't know why he'd expected Marissa to be timid but she wasn't. She was demanding and rough and he fucking loved it. With one kiss he was afraid he had become addicted. She tasted like heaven.

Gage growled in the back of his throat as he tightened his hold on her hair. She yanked at the soft black shirt he wore, trying to tug the fabric up.

He moved his mouth to her neck where he nibbled the sensitive flesh.

"Yes," she encouraged. "Yes." Kneading the muscles on his back. Dragging her nails down painfully.

Gage hissed while lifting her so she could wrap her arms and legs around him, letting her rub along the steel rod hidden by jeans.

"Please." She rubbed herself harder against him. "Please."

Gage knew he should stop the mating before it went too far, but he didn't. It wasn't his wolf in control, but the man. And the man wanted this woman under him naked, bucking, begging, and the wolf was urging him on.

"Oh, God. I'm burning for you. Please." Marissa's mouth was everywhere on him. He could swear he felt her canines lengthen as she licked and sucked his neck.

Hitching her higher around his waist, he walked deeper into the trees. They would give him plenty of cover as he took this woman.

Chapter Three

The grass met Marissa's back as Gage laid her down. His weight quickly covered her, sending electric currents through her body.

His eyes met hers briefly before he reclaimed her mouth. This kiss wasn't as forceful as the last, but more coaxing. As if he was trying to get her body to trust his. Her body didn't care about trust—it just wanted him hard and fast. She didn't want to have to think about anything other than Gage buried deep inside her.

When his mouth started to trail down, she took the opportunity to pull off his torn shirt. Well, she guessed she'd ripped that earlier. Oh well. He could probably afford another. She yanked the remaining material from his body to be able to run her palms over his hard chest. He sat up between her legs. His gaze burned into her as he slowly lifted the T-shirt. He had more control, more patience than she did, so Marissa raised her hand to help.

He slapped her hand away. "Mine," he growled at her.

She moaned, couldn't hold the sound in. Why was he turning her on so much with his dominance? She normally took control during her sexual encounters. Not this time—Gage was in control and she was wetter and hotter than she'd ever been before.

Marissa tried to close her legs in hope of relieving the ache between them, but he only spread his knees wider, moving her legs with him. If she had been naked, she would have been spread completely open for him. The way she wanted to be.

"Gage. Now. Please, now."

He bent his head and smiled at her. "Giving the Alpha orders, little one?" He ran his tongue over the silky cup of her bra. "You shall be punished for that."

That sounded like heaven to her. Whatever he wanted, just this once, she craved someone else taking control. When he licked one hard nipple through the silk, Marissa's body jerked.

"Oh, please."

Running his teeth over the opening clasp of her bra, he chuckled. "You will beg, little one. Before I am finished, you will beg." He used his teeth to tear open her bra.

Marissa thought she might explode right there when his hot, moist mouth covered her nipple. She lifted her hands to the back of his head to hold him to her. Her body screamed for more.

Without removing his mouth, he grabbed her hands and placed them over her head. "Keep your hands there," he told her before moving to the other breast and nipple.

Marissa tried—she really did—but when his body started moving down hers, her hands went automatically to his shoulders. Gage growled and nipped at her wrist. The sharp pain had her gasping and arching into him at the same time. He placed her hands back over her head and gave her a stern look, before trailing his tongue down her body.

Liquid fire slid over her, around her, and in her. Marissa desperately tried to grab onto anything to keep her hands still. Clawing at the grass and dirt, she dug her fingers in, trying to anchor herself. She'd never felt this hot, this needy. He was torturing her.

Skipping the cotton shorts she wore, Gage leisurely brought one of her legs up and ran his tongue behind her knee. She hoped her moans were telling him exactly how much she liked what he was doing. He followed the path from her knee to the edge of her shorts.

"Yes. Yes," she repeated over and over, moving her head from side to side.

Gage slowly started to peel the shorts off. The crotch was wet and she should have been embarrassed but she was past caring. As he paused to smell, she whimpered. He was undoing her with every deliberate action.

"Little wolf is dripping for me," he said, his husky voice in contrast to his slow exploration.

He wanted her, she knew that. But he was taking his sweet time.

"Yes. Yes, I am," she admitted.

He dragged her shorts all the way off then threw them behind him. With a gentle touch, he ran one finger over the crotch of her silk panties. The only barrier left on her. "Wet. So wet and hot."

Leaning over, he closed his mouth over the silk and sucked. Then, with a quick yank, he removed them.

"Oh. God. Oh. Please." Marissa moved her legs together to hold him in place.

Pressing both hands on her thighs, he opened them back up. "Do you not have any control over your body?" he teased. "Hold still."

Hold still? Was he joking? She was going to go insane.

He pulled away from her enough for her to see him. He ran his dark gaze over her body and Marissa shuddered at the look of pure lust on his face. When he sat back she could have screamed.

"Don't stop!" she demanded, desperate to feel him inside her.

Lifting that elegant eyebrow, Gage gave her an annoyed expression. "Orders again? You just can't help yourself, can you?"

Before she could respond, Marissa found herself flipped and on all fours. She dug her hands and knees into the ground again. "Yes. I mean, no. I mean… Please just take me."

Marissa felt his hard-on through the rough material of his jeans as he leaned his body over hers. "Is this what you want?"

"Yes. Oh please, yes."

Gage's hand left her, and she heard his zipper being pulled down. She prayed he was releasing himself from the confines of his jeans. Then he ran his hands along her flank and over her curves, pressing his naked body against hers. Marissa almost yowled in pleasure.

Marissa arched for him. If she could just get him inside… She started to reach back with one hand.

"No. Don't move," he ordered.

She screamed in frustration, but he only laughed at her.

"No control." Placing a kiss in the small of her back, he pulled away again.

Marissa turned her head to complain and was shocked by the feel of his hand on her ass.

Smack.

"Ahhhhhhhhh." Bracing herself with her hands, Marissa trembled. "What?"

"Need to learn manners."

Smack.

Marissa cried out again. The pain was fading into a deep pleasure that she'd never felt before.

"Need to learn restraint."

Smack. Smack.

"I… What…? No!" What was he doing to her? Should she ask him to stop? She didn't want him to but still…

"Someone should have taught you to follow orders a long time ago."

Smack.

It hurt. And it felt good. How could it feel good? She'd never been one to enjoy pain with sex, but with Gage, it seemed to fit perfectly.

Gage landed three more slaps. She lifted up each time, meeting his hand. The sharp pain only made her hotter. Made her hungrier for him. She'd never been spanked in her life. Her clit throbbed. She could taste blood from where she was biting her lip. Her mind filled with emotions she didn't understand but didn't really care about.

He stopped spanking her to rub his hands over her ass then slipped a finger between her folds, and she couldn't hold in another moan. He thrust his finger inside before pulling out and positioning himself behind her.

One hand drove into her hair and he yanked her head back as he plunged inside her willing body. He filled her completely with the first thrust, causing her to scream. She hadn't gotten a good look at his cock before, and she now knew that he was well endowed. So big and hard. Marissa wished she could have gotten her mouth on him but since he was riding her she couldn't really complain.

As he moved in and out with deep slow strokes, Marissa's body stretched to accommodate him, but the stretch felt amazing. Each time he pushed into her, she slammed herself back to meet his thrusts.

Their rhythm flowed like a dance while the speed picked up and he rode her harder. She kept her head bent and her eyes tightly closed and tried to hang on to the magical feeling of belonging. Both of his hands now held her hips tightly, his strokes growing shorter and more desperate. Unable to hold out any longer, Marissa lifted her head and cried out into the wild as her orgasm ripped through her body.

"Yes. Let me hear you," he told her, pounding inside harder.

Three more thrusts and he exploded inside her, releasing his seed deep and taking her through completion once again.

Marissa regained all her senses back slowly. The grass that she had collapsed on was wet, but she hadn't noticed earlier. Her cheek rested in a patch of dirt that her hands had been clawing at.

The weight of Gage, while heavy, was comforting. Breathing in, she held his masculine scent. She wanted to remember all of this once he abandoned her. He started to lift off her, and she barely held back a sigh at the loss of his warmth. Gage fell onto his back, but she kept her eyes closed. Her hair was probably messed and she no doubt had a sleepy, satisfied look, but she couldn't be bothered with details like that. Gage had fucked every care from her.

He surprised her by reaching over and covering her bottom with his palm. "You okay?"

"Uh-huh."

Damn if she didn't sound content and relaxed. The tension in her body seemed to have disappeared completely. When Gage leaned over and replaced his hands with his lips, she couldn't find any reason to tell him to stop. His tongue was cool against the skin of her heated flesh. Being with him had been the best sexual experience of her life.

Her eyes were still closed but Gage surprised her — using the lightest pressure, he nipped then licked at her skin. Then awareness slammed back into her.

Her eyes flew open and she lifted her head. "You *spanked* me!"

Throwing one arm over her legs to hold her in place as she tried to turn over, Gage said, "So I did."

Marissa shook her head at him. He sounded way too pleased with himself. "But…you spanked me."

Continuing to run circles over her with the tip of his tongue, he grunted his agreement.

Heat followed Gage's tongue as it traced along her body. What was going on with her? What was going on with *him*? He had to realize he had just had sex with a non-shifter. She knew some Packs encouraged relationships with humans and some kept it hidden, but she didn't know of one who would risk openly having sex with a non-shifter. And he was the Pack Alpha!

Marissa jerked away so quickly that she must have caught him by surprise, since Gage released her.

Once on her feet, she began to search around desperately for her clothes. Her shirt was next to Gage's hand. She didn't think the house was too far away, so maybe no one would see her if she ran quickly.

Gage sat, peering up at her. He watched her as if he knew

she wanted to run from him. But while she was going into full panic mode, he appeared as though it pissed him off. She couldn't worry about that, though. She had to get away.

"This what you're looking for?" He held the T-shirt out to her.

Marissa nodded and dropped her eyes. The wolf inside Gage would acknowledge the submission, but the man might not be so easily fooled.

"Well, come and get it," he challenged.

Yeah, that didn't sound like a trap, now, did it? Not like she had much of a choice if she wanted her clothes back. Marissa took a careful step toward him. She just got within arm's length of him and leaned forward to grab the shirt, and damn if he didn't grab her first. He turned quickly, holding both wrists, until she was on her back.

Following her first instinct, Marissa wiggled and fought. He only pressed more of his weight down and growled at her.

"Stop fighting me and stop moving around. I'm not hurting you," he told her.

Marissa glared at him but stopped moving.

"Now. Would you like to discuss this like adults or do you need to go over my knee?"

Despite the shiver of excitement the threat sent through her, she shook her head. "*That* is not going to happen again."

Gage leaned down until their lips were only centimeters apart. "Oh, I believe it is. I believe it's just not in you to behave."

Trying not to let his proximity cloud her mind, Marissa closed her eyes and tried to be reasonable. She took a deep breath prior to speaking again. "Gage. You don't understand."

He frowned as he gazed down at her. "About what exactly?"

"Do you know what we just did?" Her voice rose and Marissa hated that.

"I have a pretty good idea." He rubbed intimately along

her, showing her that he still had life in him yet. "Do *you* need a reminder?"

The electricity between the two of them was so hot Marissa was surprised her hair wasn't on fire.

He bent and licked her from collarbone to ear. "Have you forgotten already?"

"Oh... I..."

She didn't get any further when his mouth covered hers. With her wrists still bound in one of his hands, she was helpless to push him away or bring him closer. She was able to wrap her legs around his waist. He rubbed against her swollen wet opening as he seduced her mouth. She felt like she was drowning in emotions. She was trying, for his sake, but she was helpless to fight what she wanted. Him.

"No, you don't need a reminder, do you? You remember just fine," he said softly. Then, with his gaze holding hers, he entered her slowly.

Marissa thrust her hips up, taking him completely. "More." If they were going to be damned she might as well enjoy every second of it.

"Yes, more." Gage kept his pace slow and deep. Releasing her hands, he cupped her hips to hold them, not allowing her to set the pace.

"More. More." Marissa kept her hands pressed against the dirt like she knew he wanted.

Almost pulling completely out before slamming back in, he gave her what she needed. "This isn't something you can just ignore, Marissa."

"Just...protecting...you..." She spoke between pants as he picked up speed.

Gage raised her legs over his shoulders, taking him deeper with the next thrust. "I'm...the...Alpha." He gritted his teeth.

Her muscles gripped and massaged him each time he entered her. She was so wet, allowing him to easily pump in and out. His cock was thick and filled her with every wonderful thrust. It was almost as if her body had been made for him. Marissa knew that wasn't true, but oh how she wished it was.

As Gage slammed into her harder, Marissa cried out. Her climax came quick and fast, making her arch, taking him in farther. She milked him with her body until he was releasing inside her. Gage shook as his seed poured into her.

She basked in the feel of his claiming. It didn't mean what she secretly craved. Gage would never call her his but for the moment she could pretend.

It was a good thing she was on birth control. Things had happened so fast with Gage. Unexpected and wonderful things, but they hadn't spoken about protection. Marissa couldn't carry or pass on human diseases. That was one shifter gene she did carry but pregnancy would be a huge issue. An Alpha having a baby with a non-shifter? They'd both be killed.

Gage was still inside her with his arms braced to keep his full weight from crushing her. He didn't seem to be thinking about anything at all.

It worried her that Gage would be so reckless.

His Pack needed him to stay strong and lead them. By being with her he wasn't just putting himself in danger but all of them.

When he started to nuzzle her neck, she closed her eyes and sighed. She'd just managed to complicate things beyond what she would be able to control. She had to think of some way to save them all.

Chapter Four

"Marissa..." Gage didn't know what to say to express his feelings. To tell her that she was his. It was too soon but he knew it, his wolf agreed, and fate had brought the two of them together. She would fight him, but he would never let her go.

He could offer her so much if she'd just accept him. There was a reason he was the Alpha of the largest Pack in Texas. He was strong and could protect those who trusted him with their lives. Marissa would be included in that group.

Reaching up, she cupped his cheek.

His heart twisted in happiness at her intimate gesture.

"I'm not trying to be difficult here, but by being with me..." she started.

Gage caught a familiar scent and stiffened as his head snapped up. Now was not the time for visitors.

"What?" Marissa pushed at his chest.

Standing, Gage pulled Marissa up with him. "Someone's coming." He didn't know how in tune she was with her senses but she should be aware someone was walking up on them. Maybe she didn't have enhanced hearing?

"Who?" She went in search for her clothes once again. Her shirt was right beside where she'd been lying. She blushed as she picked it up.

After what they'd done he didn't know why she'd be embarrassed but it was endearing. Shifters were used to seeing one another without clothing and although she didn't change herself she'd still been born in a Pack.

"I know who it is and they are deliberately making enough noise so we hear them."

"So they know we're here?"

Turning around, Gage smiled at her reassuringly before he kissed her forehead. She was worried and he wanted to assure her that everything would be okay but he doubted she would believe him. Damn it, a little more time and he would have been able to convince her that she should go back to the main house with him. "Your shorts are tangled in the tree root."

He watched as she pulled her shorts and shirt on quickly. She peeked over at him, and he didn't miss the look of hunger in her eyes. Then she glanced toward his clothes in a silent message. Gage wasn't in any hurry to put them back on and wished she hadn't been either. It wasn't like the Pack hadn't seen him naked before. They did shift and go on runs together.

"Gage."

"You have a great body."

"Gage. Someone is coming," she whispered with a look of horror on her face.

"They're already here." Turning, he faced his second in command.

Logan kept his eyes down and his smile hidden as he faced his Alpha. Gage saw it but hoped Marissa remained out of view. He didn't want the teasing that Logan would give him to make her uncomfortable.

Now thinking more clearly, Gage was glad Marissa had covered herself up. He didn't want anyone else to see her.

"Alpha," Logan greeted, dipping his head respectfully. Gage knew it was more for Marissa than him.

He crossed his arms over his chest. "Logan."

Marissa had moved behind him even though she had pulled her clothes on.

"I...uh... Elizabeth came home to have lunch with her sister and got worried when she wasn't in the house. She called up to the main house so I came over...to...uh."

"Oh, God." Marissa dropped her forehead onto Gage's back.

Gage saw Logan unsuccessfully try to smother a laugh. "We'll be right up."

Nodding, Logan started to back off.

"Take the short way," Gage ordered.

Logan had obviously circled around so he could make sure they heard him. If he'd come straight from Elizabeth's there would have been a good chance of him running right into them. He appreciated his friend's compassion for Marissa.

Marissa kept her face hidden in Gage's back until Logan passed. "Oh, God."

"Relax." Stepping away, Gage bent down and grabbed his jeans. "We're adults."

Her face was red and she kept her gaze on the ground. "I am so sorry. I didn't know she was coming home," she mumbled, but he heard her clearly.

Gage shrugged into what was left of his shirt. "Wouldn't have mattered. Once I saw you standing at the edge of the trees, I would have had you anyway."

She didn't respond to his announcement but turned away. "Have you seen my panties and bra?"

Recognizing the change in subject, Gage decided to let it go for now. "Bra's by the tree, although I believe it's toast."

Marissa picked it up. "Panties?"

Gage pulled them out of his pocket. "They were under my pants."

Marissa held her hand out.

Gage just smiled at her and stuffed them back in his pocket.

"Gage."

"Come on." He reached out for her hand and tugged her toward the house.

"Gage, give them to me."

"No."

"Why do you want them? Some kind of trophy?"

Laughing, he continued to tow her. "Whatever you want to think, Marissa." He couldn't very well tell her that they smelled like her and he planned to carry them with him at all times he was away from her. That might make her freak out even more than she already was.

"Just don't see why you'd want to keep them," she complained but didn't say anything else.

He grabbed her hand then hauled her after him. They would straighten all of this out then hopefully he could talk Marissa into having a quiet dinner with him later. He knew she needed to spend time with her sister but Gage didn't want to be away from her for long. And he always got what he wanted.

It would be a point of pride for him to show her around the Alpha house and introduce her to his Pack. Marissa would make a great partner for him and her strength would benefit the Pack.

Gage could already picture her fitting right in.

They were close, the entire Pack. Ever since his dad had left them in his care, Gage had made sure to be a good and fair Alpha. His dad had led them for so long that any change in leadership would have been difficult, but Gage felt like the transition had been smooth.

His father now sat on the Wolf Council that ruled over all wolf shifters in the United States. Gage was so proud of him and hoped that he'd be able to come down soon to meet Marissa.

She was quiet on the short walk back to Elizabeth's. Gage knew she was embarrassed but as a shifter she really should have been used to being exposed to outdoor sex. It was natural for what they were.

Walking into the house, Marissa felt a new wave of embarrassment. Not only was her sister there but also the man from the woods and Elizabeth's mate. Marissa tried to pull her hand away, but Gage tightened his grip.

"Marissa, I was worried when you weren't in the house and didn't leave a note. I'm sorry I..."

Again Marissa attempted to pull her hand away but

couldn't. "It's okay, Elizabeth," she aimed to assure her sister.

How could she explain to her sister in a room full of strangers that the mistake was her own? She didn't want Elizabeth blaming herself. Marissa was the one to mess everything up. All she had to do was control herself and she couldn't even do that. Two days and she was already breaking laws.

"No. I shouldn't have called up to the main house…"

"Elizabeth, it's fine." Marissa waved a hand — unfortunately, it was the hand still holding her torn bra.

Elizabeth gasped as Logan and Greg laughed out loud. Marissa wished the floor would just open up and swallow her. Would the embarrassment never end?

Whipping her hand behind her back, Marissa pulled on the other one, and Gage finally released her. When she would have run upstairs, he put a firm arm around her waist and held her in place.

But instead of making excuses about what had obviously happened, Gage just hugged her tight against him. Knowing he needed a way out, she tried to come up with anything she could to get rid of him.

"I need to take a shower," Marissa said to no one in particular. She was surprised when Gage smiled down at her and turned to the others. He knew what she was doing. It was obvious by the look on his face. Why he wasn't freaking out Marissa didn't know. Maybe since he was the Alpha he didn't feel like he needed to follow the rules? That didn't seem like the man she'd gotten to know but, really, she didn't know him at all. Sure, he was kind and compassionate as well as being a great lover, but that didn't tell her anything about how he ran his Pack.

"Gentlemen, why don't we leave the ladies to clean up and have lunch?"

Marissa was grateful he wasn't fighting her on this. If she could get a few minutes to think it would all be okay.

She was beyond relieved when everyone agreed and the

men headed for the door.

"I will see you later tonight, Marissa," he whispered in her ear before releasing her and walking away. "We'll have dinner at my house." No, they wouldn't, but Marissa wasn't about to argue in front of everyone else.

Marissa waited for the front door to close before lifting her head. Her sister stood with her arms crossed over her chest and a look of disapproval written all over her face.

"Don't," she warned Elizabeth.

"You didn't learn the first time?" Elizabeth asked, concern evident in her tone and in the softening of her expression.

"It was an accident."

"An accident?" her sister repeated with no amusement. "Tell me, just how do you accidentally get naked and have sex with the Pack Alpha?"

"How do you know I had sex with him?"

Elizabeth just lifted a brow.

"Okay, fine, I had sex with him." Marissa started to walk out of the room.

"Why?" Elizabeth asked, following.

"It's not like I planned it." She couldn't explain it to Elizabeth until she was able to explain it to herself.

"Marissa, he is my Alpha." Elizabeth's voice rose, and it reminded Marissa of when they were kids and Marissa had once again gotten herself in some sort of trouble. Guilt replaced everything else she had been feeling.

"I know."

"I can't believe you did this."

The disappointment she heard doubled the guilt Marissa already felt. Reaching the guestroom, she pushed the door open. "You know, he did have a say in the matter."

"Yes, he did." Elizabeth sighed. "I'm sorry, but you know what happened last time. This is my Pack, and that is my Alpha. I won't let you ruin this for me."

That hurt. She knew Elizabeth had every reason to be angry but why was it always what Marissa wanted that caused trouble? When Marissa turned, her eyes filled with tears. "I didn't mean to ruin anything."

Elizabeth's sigh was audible. "You know that male wolves for some reason think they are above the law. I'm sure Gage wasn't thinking about it at the time, but you should have been."

Marissa *knew* she should have. "I'm sure he thought he would be able to keep it quiet. Brandon always told me not to tell anyone about us and I'm sure that's what Gage will tell me later."

"If this got out..." Elizabeth took a step back and had tears in her eyes.

Marissa shouldn't have come. She'd just turned the best time of Elizabeth's life into a horrible situation.

"I'm sorry, Elizabeth." Marissa couldn't be any sorrier for her actions. Once again, she would be responsible for them losing everything.

"I know." Elizabeth reached out and pulled her close.

Marissa dropped her head onto her sister's shoulder while they hugged. At least she still had her family.

"It's not fair," Elizabeth said then drew back. "But we know how life isn't fair. I shouldn't have asked you to come. It was selfish of me."

"No," Marissa assured her. "My fault."

Her sister sent her a sad smile. "Maybe it would be best if you left. Tonight."

"Okay." Turning toward the bathroom, Marissa felt the first tear fall. It *would* be best. For everyone concerned.

The bathroom was small but Marissa liked it. Not too much room. She slid down against the wall and let her tears fall freely.

She was a freak and no one could help her.

Once she gained control over her emotions, she climbed to her feet then crossed to the sink and the hanging mirror. She glared at her reflection.

Her hair was messed up and had grass and a few twigs tangled in. While her eyes were red rimmed she couldn't hide the fact that she'd been crying. It didn't matter, though.

She wouldn't see anyone else.

Instead of trying to change her departure date, maybe she should just drive home. It would give her time to think about things. Time to work out why she always messed everything up.

Turning, she walked over to the shower then turned on the water. She needed to get Gage's scent off her. There was no point in torturing herself with his memory.

* * * *

"We have a problem." Logan walked into the Alpha's office without knocking.

"What?" Gage looked up from the papers in front of him. He was trying to concentrate on the Pack's financial books while he organized a family gathering for a couple of weeks away. The annual get-together would be the perfect time to introduce Marissa to his Pack.

"Greg just called. Elizabeth sent Marissa home."

"She what?" Gage's voice rose as he jumped up.

Logan took a step back. "After we left, Elizabeth sent Marissa back to California. Greg doesn't know why but said Elizabeth's upset. He called me as soon as he found out. Marissa's probably already to the gate."

No!

Yanking up the phone, Gage had to control his temper to keep from crushing the piece of plastic. He punched in the number he needed. This couldn't be happening. He'd finally found the woman that he wanted to claim as his own and she was about to slip through his fingers.

"Guardhouse," the guard on duty answered.

"Tom. Has Marissa Boyd driven through yet?" Gage asked, praying he wasn't too late.

"No, Alpha. No one's been through for about fifteen minutes, and that was Sammy and Kyle."

He was able to breathe again. Marissa was still on his property. "She doesn't leave," Gage told him.

"But—"

"Don't let her out," he ordered. "I'm on my way." Slamming down the phone, he turned to Logan. "Get Elizabeth up here now. We're going to get to the bottom of this once and for all. Something else is going on."

Logan nodded and backed out of the room.

Gage ran over to the sliding glass door and opened it so hard it bounced back a little. He was probably lucky that the glass didn't shatter. Not that he cared. He could shift and get there faster but then he'd be in his wolf form and didn't want to scare Marissa.

He didn't know how she'd react.

No, he had to trust his guard to follow his order and keep Marissa inside until Gage could get there.

Gage did run, though. He could make it to the gate in less than five minutes if he used his full speed. Thankfully, shifters were faster even in their human form.

"What do you mean I can't leave?" Marissa banged her fist on the steering wheel. She shouldn't have been surprised. She'd known Gage wasn't finished with her. She just didn't know how he'd found out so fast. There was no way that Elizabeth would have called him. Her sister was trying to fix things the only way she knew how.

Gage wouldn't understand but that wasn't their problem. Male wolf shifters always thought they could get away with anything. Why he couldn't see that she was protecting him was beyond her, but she really didn't need this shit. She wanted out.

"Open the gate!" she ordered the poor guard. It really wasn't his fault but he was the one in her way. She felt panic start to rise inside her. If she saw Gage again it would be so hard to leave.

"I'm sorry, ma'am, but I have orders you are not to leave territory."

"I don't care what your orders are. I'm not a Pack member and you can't keep me here. I know the rules," she said.

"I'm sorry, ma'am."

"Listen here, let me out!" she pleaded almost desperately. She had to get out of there. It was best for the Pack. They had to understand that.

"No, he won't."

Marissa jumped as Gage came around the side of the car. "What the hell are you doing here?" she asked, although she knew. Still, she could play dumb and act like everything was okay. Hell, she could even lie and say she was going for a drive.

One glance at the tightness on Gage's face banished that thought. He couldn't be easily played.

Gage nodded to his guard, who appeared relieved to be dismissed from dealing with her.

"Where are you going?" Gage kept his voice low and calm. His eyes were hard as he glared at her.

She looked away from him. Guilt and shame kept her from meeting his gaze. She didn't want to be submissive to him but the power that was radiating off him was almost choking. And was messing with her. Even angry he was devastatingly handsome and her pussy grew wet. If he was any closer he'd probably be able to smell her arousal. This was exactly what she'd been afraid of.

"I asked you where you were going," he said sharply.

Tightening her hands on the wheel, Marissa kept staring straight ahead. "Home."

Gage yanked the car door open. "Move over."

"No." Was that her voice? Husky and full of need?

His hands were gentle as he unbuckled her seat belt. Marissa could tell he was angry but he wasn't hurting her as he pushed her toward the passenger seat. Since she didn't have any choice, she climbed over the console as Gage dropped down into the spot she'd just left. Surprise over took her that she'd given up in so easy. Damn, the man messed with her head.

"Hey! Hey! You can't do this!" She grabbed at his wrists and hands. She grew desperate. She scratched at his flesh but he ignored her attempts at getting him away and put the car in reverse.

"Gage, stop!"

When the road was wide enough, he turned the car and headed back toward the houses.

"Gage, please stop." She didn't want to fight with him. She just wanted to forget everything. Maybe if she could just stop anything else from happening she could go home, lick her wounds, and never think about Gage again. She slapped the dash in frustration. "Let me leave, please. On my own. I promise not to come back."

"Let you leave?" His voice rose. "Do you really think I'm just going to let you take off without a word?"

"This isn't about you, Gage. I... I just have to leave."

"No. You're not running, Marissa."

"She asked me to leave!" Marissa shouted. It hurt to tell him that but it was the truth and she couldn't keep it in. She swallowed. She was so confused. As much as she was fighting him she wanted him to tell her it would be okay. How screwed up was she?

Gage glanced over at her as he navigated the road. "Because of me."

Marissa looked away. He already knew so why had he even asked? If Marissa couldn't control herself around him then she had to put as much distance between them as possible.

"That's what I thought."

She sat quietly next to Gage. She didn't have anything more to say. If she gave him the chance to order her not to tell anyone about their encounter then she'd be able to leave. All she had to do was try to keep how much his words would hurt from being obvious and she could get on with her life. Marissa crossed her arms over her chest and took deep breaths. She'd make her escape soon and never cross back into Texas again.

* * * *

Elizabeth sat with her hands in her lap, nervously rubbing them together. She hadn't expected Gage to take her sister's leaving well, but being ordered to his office was a shock. Guilt still ate at her stomach and she hated that Marissa's visit had come to this.

It wasn't Marissa's fault and Elizabeth knew that. Elizabeth wasn't only sending Marissa back to California to get her away from trouble. She also couldn't stand to see Marissa hurt again.

All their lives Marissa had taken the brunt of hatred from shifters. Just because her sister couldn't shift had made everyone from their birth Pack turn on her. It wasn't fair and Marissa had tried to fit in. Elizabeth hadn't known how to help. She still didn't.

All she knew was that if Marissa got involved with another shifter it would destroy her, and Elizabeth couldn't let that happen.

She glared at her future mate, who stood next to the bar talking quietly with Logan. Greg had called Logan after Elizabeth had explained why Marissa had left. Greg hadn't been happy either. Didn't they understand she was trying to protect them and everyone in the Pack as well as her sister?

She jumped up when Gage walked in with her sister in tow. Gage looked pissed off and she knew that wouldn't bode well for them. Elizabeth pushed down the feeling of resentment toward her Alpha. He'd been a better Alpha than she could have hoped for. The fact that he'd given in to his needs without thought about how that would affect Marissa hurt and disappointed her.

"Sit," he snapped at Marissa, pointing to a chair.

Marissa started to refuse until Gage turned those fierce gray eyes on her. Elizabeth would have been trembling under that look but not her sister.

With a huff, Marissa lowered herself into the wingback

chair with her back to the window. It appeared that Marissa was also aware that Gage was past the point of being reasonable. It would be up to Elizabeth to smooth things over. Hopefully she wouldn't get kicked out of the Pack as well. She really did love Greg and wanted to make a life with him.

"Out," he ordered the two men.

She wanted to call out to her future mate but knew that wouldn't help matters. Even though she was upset with Greg she still needed his reassurance.

Gage nodded at Elizabeth to sit. Once she was settled back on the couch, he sat behind his desk. Elizabeth tried to catch her sister's eyes but Marissa wouldn't look at her.

Elizabeth really should have handled the situation better, explained what was best, but she was scared Gage wouldn't let her mate with Greg now. She'd almost lost her position once in a Pack because of her sister. Of course, that blame didn't fall completely on Marissa. She'd been young and in love, and Elizabeth couldn't fault her for what had been out of her control.

"Explain." Gage looked at her, speaking quietly.

Elizabeth ran her sweaty hands over her pants. She needed to take charge of the conversation and hopefully salvage her standing while still managing to protect Marissa. "I believe it's best if Marissa leaves."

"Because of what happened earlier between her and me?"

"She doesn't belong in Pack territory." Her heart almost broke at the sound of Marissa's breath catching. She didn't want to hurt her sister, but she didn't have much choice. The harsh words would make Gage understand.

"Yet you asked permission for me to let her come. Now you want her to go?"

"Well, I didn't know… I mean, I…" She didn't know what he wanted her to say.

Gage nodded before glancing at Marissa. "How do you feel?"

Marissa's face was blank and her eyes had turned cold. It

was an expression Elizabeth hadn't seen on her sister's face since she'd left their former Pack.

"I was leaving, wasn't I?" Marissa told him, her face and tone not giving away any feelings.

"Just like that?" Gage continued to speak calmly. When Marissa didn't answer him, he looked back at Elizabeth. "I'm beginning to think I have missed some important information about your old Pack."

"I told you everything, Alpha. I didn't hide anything!" This was it. He was going to kick her out. Tell her she couldn't mate with Greg.

Instead, he peered back at Marissa. "In the woods, you said you were trying to protect me."

Marissa glared at him. "Yeah, so?"

"Protect me from what?"

She didn't answer. Elizabeth was used to her sister's attitude but could see Gage was losing patience. Marissa was falling back on what she knew. Stay silent, take your punishment, and show no weakness. It was a lesson they both knew well. Still, maybe Elizabeth could help. She opened her mouth to answer, but Gage cut his gaze to her and shook his head. Elizabeth closed her mouth and stared at her sister. Marissa still wouldn't look at her.

"And you will harm me, Marissa?" Gage asked as they both watched Marissa.

Marissa only shrugged. Elizabeth wanted to come to her sister's defense, but knew she couldn't help her if Gage wouldn't even let her talk.

"Answer the question," Gage said louder, making Marissa press back into the chair.

"The law," she finally told him.

"What law?" Gage glanced from Marissa to Elizabeth with a confused look.

Marissa crossed her arms over her chest in response.

Gage peered over at Elizabeth.

"The one against mating with a non-shifter," Elizabeth answered.

"The law against mating with a non-shifter," Gage repeated.

Marissa jumped up from her seat. "Can I leave now?"

"Sit down!" he barked though he didn't raise his voice.

Elizabeth almost fell over in shock when her sister dropped back down into her chair. No one, not even their former Alpha, had been able to get that reaction from her.

"Who told you about this law?" Gage asked Elizabeth, since it was obvious Marissa wasn't going to contribute to this conversation.

"Our Alpha," Elizabeth answered.

His gaze never left her sister's face. "And what did he tell you would happen?"

"Because she... She was..."

"Because I fucked his son, not only could I be kicked out of the Pack but so could my entire family," Marissa exploded, jumping up and smashing her hand onto his desk.

Elizabeth jumped, but Gage didn't show any reaction.

"And were you all?" Gage asked, even though he knew the answer.

"I agreed to leave and never return so my sister still had a Pack to protect her," Marissa answered, anger burning in her eyes.

He rose and came around the desk. She didn't step back but stood straight when he stepped in front of her. She was bracing herself but he didn't know against what. Things started to click together for him. If he could go back and save her from her past he would.

"So can I go?" Marissa snapped. "I think it goes without saying I won't be mentioning this to anyone."

"Marissa." He wanted to hold her. To comfort her.

"I'm willing to go now so you don't have to kick her out. No one else needs to know. I'll leave quietly," she told him.

She peeked up at him. She was pleading with him and he couldn't believe how much pain showed in her gaze.

Gage gently cupped her cheek, but she jerked away from

him. "I'm sorry for everything you have been through."

Marissa remained stiff so he turned back toward Elizabeth. "While it may have been that Pack's rule, it is in no way a law. I have never heard of anything more ridiculous."

"If that's true, then..." Elizabeth trailed off, and Gage knew she was piecing together that they had been lied to. She paled. Yes, Elizabeth had figured it out.

"It's true," he assured her, then glanced back at Marissa. Reaching for her, he drew her to his side.

"Then Marissa didn't have to leave." Elizabeth also stood. "She didn't have to be on her own all this time?"

He watched the play of emotions on Marissa's face before her eyes chilled again and she pulled away. "You don't know what you are talking about." Her voice was barely above a whisper.

Gage shook his head. "Why do you think we have a council of former Alphas to police the Packs? It's to protect the members, not to hurt them." He could see Marissa starting to shake in front of him. "My father is one of the Council members and I can assure you that, whether you can shift or not, he would have never allowed you to be mistreated. There is no such law."

"It *is* a law!" Marissa yelled.

He knew she wasn't trying to convince him but had to come to terms with it. No Alpha would let such a young woman live alone and unprotected if he could help it. Gage was already making plans to research into her old Pack.

"I can prove it to you if that's what it takes," Gage said. "One call and we can have all this sorted out." It was what he could offer her, although he didn't think that she would take him up on it.

"No," she whispered. Her eyes started to swim with tears, and Gage's heart broke for her.

"Oh, Marissa, I'm so sorry." Elizabeth moved toward her.

Marissa held up a hand to stop her at the same time as stepping away from him. "Whatever. It doesn't matter."

She would need time to get used to the truth. He wouldn't

let her go through it alone, though. Whether or not she wanted his help, Gage was going to be there to support her.

Elizabeth glanced at him and he nodded toward the door. "Go out and find Greg. We'll finish up here and I'll drive Marissa back to your house."

"Marissa has her own car. And it's already packed," Marissa interjected.

Gage didn't even look back at her but kept his gaze on her sister. "She'll be okay here with me."

"Okay... I'll...see you both later." Elizabeth quickly made her exit.

The office was quiet and he could hear each breath that Marissa took. Her hands shook as though she was attempting to hang on to her control.

"Come here, baby," Gage ordered gently.

Marissa shook her head. "I want to leave."

Gage closed the distance between them then wrapped his arms around her. "Yes, I think you do. But not yet," he told her. "That's not the answer."

"No." Marissa tried to pull away. "Now. I want to leave now."

"It's okay, baby." Gage held her tight as the tears she'd been fighting started to fall.

She remained stiff until a sob overtook her.

Gage kissed her forehead then turned her face into his chest. "You're not alone any longer."

"I can't..." she managed before the dam broke.

As she cried in his arms, anger swelled inside him at the Alpha who had pledged to take care of her then turned her out without a Pack, without her family. To put her through hell for her being with his son. It should have been a relationship worth celebrating.

Gage hummed to her, trying to comfort her in any way he could.

It seemed she pulled back, tears still streaming down her face as she looked up at him. He wasn't surprised when she pressed her lips to his in a desperate kiss. Marissa was trying to replace the agony with anything else. Glad to be able to take some of the pain away, he let her kiss him and tightened his hold around her.

His cock was already hard, had been even through his anger, since he'd climbed into the car with her.

With one hand holding her back, he ran his other down to cup her ass. She shuffled her feet and drew even closer to him. Gage plunged his tongue in and out of her mouth like he wanted to do with his cock inside her pussy.

If Marissa needed to forget he would be more than happy to take her mind and body to better things.

Chapter Five

Marissa pressed herself close to Gage. His body was strong, solid and everything she needed right now. If she just didn't have to think then everything would be okay. She could forget the betrayal and pain from finding out that her entire adult life had been built on a lie.

Gage's arm tightened around her as he kissed her back. The hand under her ass helped her lift her leg to wrap it around his waist. That put her in the perfect position to feel his hard-on against her. When he pulled away and looked at her, Marissa's heart skipped. He was so attractive, and even if she didn't know why he wanted her she'd take it for now.

She could get used to this man being there for her. And that was scary. Even if what he'd said was true, that didn't mean her life would be any different. She was still a non-shifter in a world where she didn't truly belong.

"Please," she pleaded as she rubbed her hand down his chest. She needed him to make her stop thinking.

"Upstairs. I want you in my bed," he whispered in her ear. "I want to make love to you for hours."

Why did they have to leave the office? Didn't he realize that she would give in to him right there? What if someone saw them together on the way to his room?

"Once I get you in my bed you'll stay there," he told her. "Mine to do with whatever I want."

Marissa shivered at his declaration. No more hiding. No shame in being with a wolf. She didn't have to hold back her needs with him. She wasn't sure if she could give him what he wanted but she could try. "Okay, upstairs."

Gage took her mouth again, this time with more force. Marissa gave herself to him willingly. He lifted her off her feet easily and she wrapped her arms and both legs around him.

"We'll also talk about your punishment for talking back to me. Again."

Marissa shuddered with excitement as she scraped her teeth over his neck. She wanted punishment even if she didn't want to say the words. "Maybe later."

Gage chuckled. He must have caught how much she craved it.

They barely made it up to his room without her ripping his clothes off. Luckily they didn't run into anyone to slow them down. Marissa would have been horrified if a Pack member had seen how desperate she was for him. It wasn't only the fact that he was taking her mind off things. She wanted to enjoy being with him without the familiar guilt she always felt. This would be the first time she gave herself to another shifter without the fear of discovery.

Gage kicked his bedroom door closed as Marissa teased him with her tongue on his neck and ear. He stumbled slightly before he caught himself, and she liked that she was affecting him so much.

When he dropped her carelessly onto the bed, Marissa bounced, laughing while looking around. "Oh wow." It was a great bedroom. Worthy of an Alpha.

Gage already had his shirt over his head. "Yeah. Strip."

Ignoring him, Marissa knelt on the giant bed and took in her surroundings. "This room is huge."

Although there were no lights on, she could see clearly enough. The bed was up two steps on a platform. To her left were balcony doors with the curtains tied open and to her right a sitting area with couch, table and chairs, and a flat-screen TV. A door on the far wall would probably lead to a bathroom. The entire space was done in shades of gray.

"You're not undressed," Gage practically growled at her.

Marissa looked at him and took in the naked body in front

of her. Lean and muscular. Tan with no lines. She made quick work of removing her clothes then scooted closer on her knees. "Your room distracted me. Now you have distracted me." She licked a small circle on his chest.

Gage pulled her back by her hair. "You've been distracting me since the first moment I laid eyes on you. Now lie back."

The urge to follow his command was strong but she needed something different this time. She hoped he understood. Marissa pressed a kiss into his chest. "Please let me do this, Gage." She needed to feel in control. Since first arriving, she had felt like her life was spiraling around her and she was only a passenger.

His eyes softened, telling her he understood. "Okay, baby."

She reached out and yanked him onto the bed. He let her lay him on his back then she straddled his waist. Marissa took her time kissing Gage's lips, running her teeth over his neck and chin, before lavishing his chest with more kisses. Keeping his hands at his sides, he allowed her to explore his body. *And what a body it was.* She breathed in his scent. Rich, dark and male. She rubbed against him as she traveled down. She was getting his scent all over her and that was making her even hotter.

"Marissa." Gage tried to pull her back up, moving his hands into her hair, but she continued to lower herself to the object she wanted most. His gorgeous, fully erect cock. Licking from the base up, she felt him let out a rush of breath. Then, with just the tip of her tongue, she teased the head.

"Marissa," Gage hissed out, raising his head to look down at her.

Oh, she could definitely get used to this. She opened and took him into her mouth. Gage groaned and dropped his head back down. Adding her hand, she stroked and sucked him deeper into the back of her throat. He was salty and she loved it as his hips bucked to press him farther into her mouth.

"That's it. Suck me, baby," he murmured to her approvingly.

Marissa did. Tipping her head back, she took him as far as she could while sucking him hard.

"Stop," he ordered.

She hummed and swallowed, trying to push him over the edge. To make him lose control like he seemed to manage with her.

"Stop!"

Marissa gave him one last lick before looking up. He stared down at her. His eyes glowed, showing just how close she had been to making him lose control and spill into her mouth.

"Come here," he commanded.

She didn't see any reason not to get what she wanted — him inside her.

She rubbed up him slowly, arousing both of them with the brush of her body on his. When she was straddling his thighs once more, he gripped her hips. Marissa took Gage's hard cock in her hand and teased her pussy lips with it. Moaning, she continued to torment them both until he growled.

That sound traveled down her spine until she thought she might come before he even got in her. She took just the tip of him, biting her bottom lip, trying to control her need. Sliding down slowly so her body could adjust to his girth, she placed her palm on his chest. When he was fully inside, she rocked forward.

Gage moaned, or maybe it was her — she couldn't tell anymore. He felt so good filling her. As if he was the only one who belonged there. Still gripping her, he began to thrust up to meet her every time she rocked. Marissa cried out, throwing her head back. She rode him faster as his hips lifted to meet her. Gage matched her speed, pulling her down harder each time.

"Yes." Marissa leaned forward, her hair falling over both of them, making a curtain around them.

She was almost there. That sweet release was only a few strokes from taking her. They rocked in a rhythm that built in intensity, but it wasn't enough.

Gage slipped an arm around her waist and she knew what was going to happen. When he flipped her onto her back, Marissa pleaded at him with her eyes to finish her off. He must have felt the need for more, too, because he slammed and pounded into her harder. She could take it, loved it. No human lover could ever match the way a shifter could move.

"Oh, oh," Marissa panted. She was there, ready to explode.

"Stay with me," Gage grunted out, plunging inside incredibly fast and hard.

Marissa's body spasmed. Reaching up, she grabbed his arms. "Yes. More."

Roaring as if his control was gone, he took her not only as a man takes a woman but also as a wolf would take his mate. She was still screaming when the first orgasm passed and another hit stronger, taking all her breath away. Gage threw his head back and yelled out his own release before collapsing on top of her.

* * * *

The day of the ceremony was busy for both Elizabeth and Marissa. Marissa took extra time to help her sister get ready — drawing Elizabeth a hot scented bath, fixing her hair and makeup before helping her dress.

"That dress is beautiful. *You* are beautiful," Marissa told her sister, trying to hold back the tears. For the first time that she could ever remember the tears were good and not from pain. Elizabeth was shining and to Marissa she had never been more beautiful as she was at that moment.

Her loose white dress brought out her natural coloring and flowed around her curves. Marissa straightened one of Elizabeth's straps before she stood back to just admire her.

Elizabeth was bouncing on her toes. "I can't believe it's

finally here. I'm going to perform the mating ceremony."

Marissa leaned over and kissed her sister's cheek. "Not if you don't hurry."

Laughing, Elizabeth twirled around. "I'm ready."

Taking her hand, Marissa smiled. "Then I'd better get you there."

As she started to lead her from the room, Elizabeth pulled her back. "I'm sorry," she said quietly.

"There's nothing to be sorry about," Marissa assured, and meant it. They hadn't spoken about what Gage had revealed, instead concentrating on the ceremony and enjoying each other's company. It had been wonderful to relax, laugh and talk without having anything hanging over their heads. She'd hoped they could get through the day without the subject being brought up.

Elizabeth stood in front of her, and Marissa knew that regardless of how long she had avoided this talk, it was going to happen now. Or her sister wouldn't go.

"I love you," Marissa started, going with honesty. "I will admit that over the years I've been jealous of you. I didn't want to be different. I wanted to be either a were or a human."

"Oh, honey."

Marissa shook her head, cutting off Elizabeth's sympathy. "No. It's not your fault and it's not mine. Talking with Gage and Logan, I realized we both had a bad deal. We both deserved a better Pack than we got."

"If I'd have known…"

Marissa hugged her then cupped her cheek. "But you didn't. Please, I want to give you this day. I want everything to be perfect for you. I'm okay."

"But…"

"I'm okay, Elizabeth. Please believe me." Marissa needed Elizabeth to drop it. If she kept busy and let Elizabeth's happiness fill her she didn't have to think of everything she'd missed out on.

"Okay." Elizabeth took a deep breath and Marissa was

glad her sister hadn't cried. They didn't have time to fix her makeup. They were already late.

"So, let's go!" Marissa ushered her toward the door.

Elizabeth smiled but didn't move. "One more question."

She knew what was coming. Even knowing didn't help with the answer.

"What about you and Gage?" Elizabeth asked.

"I don't know." Marissa could only tell her the truth. The last few days with Gage had been wonderful but also confusing. She wanted the Alpha more each time they were together. It was like she couldn't get enough of him. For an independent woman who'd never given a thought to settling down, her relationship with Gage confused her.

"But you do care about him."

"I do," she admitted. "But I'm not a Pack member. I don't belong here. I have to go home soon." It was the first time she'd spoken the words out loud and they broke her heart. Still, the reality was that she had a home to return to. Even though Gage kept mentioning a gathering with his Pack, Marissa knew she wouldn't be there. Couldn't.

"You could stay. Be part of the Pack. We could be close again." Elizabeth spoke of everything Marissa had already thought about.

"I can't. I'm sorry, but I just can't," Marissa told her softly. She really didn't want to have this conversation. "Please don't let this ruin your day."

Elizabeth smiled but it didn't reach her eyes. "No. I won't let anything ruin today. I just wish you'd think about staying."

"What if I promise to visit more?"

Finally Elizabeth's smile reached her eyes and lit up her face. "Are you going to be coming to see me or Gage?" she teased.

Marissa laughed. "Good question." But did she know the answer? What if after she left, Gage never wanted to see her again? Marissa couldn't handle any more rejection. As much as she was trying to keep things light between them, she hadn't managed to do so.

The previous night after they'd made love, Gage had wrapped his arms tight around her and she'd just gazed at him until she'd fallen asleep. The feeling of being safe and protected was so foreign that she never wanted to be without it. Still, Gage was an Alpha. He had an entire Pack to take care of and that meant one day providing cubs for a future generation.

There was no way Marissa would be able to give him children. The chance that they would be non-shifters was something she wouldn't be able to deal with. Because of her own limited abilities, she'd never bring a baby into a world that had been so cruel to her. Gage deserved a woman that'd be able to give him and the Pack strong shifters.

As she followed Elizabeth out of the door, Marissa tried to push all her insecurities down. These worries didn't belong. She needed to enjoy the limited time she had left. That would allow her to live the rest of her life without any regrets.

* * * *

Gage paced his office while Logan sat back comfortably on the couch.

"Nervous?"

"Of course I'm not nervous," Gage growled. This wasn't the first time he'd performed the mating ceremony. Almost like a human marriage ceremony, the mating forever ceremony just had more detail added by the shifters. A wolf in the wild only took one mate. That was how his Pack took their own vows. No matter what came up in the future, the mating between two shifters would hold strong.

"She sure is something."

"Yes, she is. Everyone loves Elizabeth." Gage knew that Logan didn't have a thing for Elizabeth so he didn't know what his second was getting at.

"I wasn't talking about her."

Gage stopped in front of him, noting the smug look Logan had. "What?" he questioned. Then he knew. Gage rolled his eyes. Logan had been on at him about getting a commitment from Marissa but Gage was trying not to push her. So he was being very careful.

"Have you talked to Marissa about staying longer?"

Gage went back to pacing. He'd tried to talk to her about Pack life. After all, committing to the Pack wasn't committing to him. But she'd changed the subject when he'd brought it up. She was due to leave the next day. Every time they were alone together, he broached the subject. And she successfully distracted him.

"So you're just going to let her go?" Logan shook his head.

Gage knew he was only trying to help. There was a reason Logan was his second. The Pack respected him because he was fair, and Logan was like a dog with a bone. Never giving up on something he believed in.

"Maybe you don't deserve her then if you're just going to let her go."

"Watch your step, Logan," Gage warned.

"Excuse me, Alpha, but you are more than just my leader. You're my friend. I haven't seen you this relaxed...this happy in years," Logan pleaded. "And we both know it's because of her."

Gage walked across the room to stare out of the window onto the grounds of his territory. His home. He loved it there and knew if Marissa gave the place and him a chance she would find her own happiness.

When he'd seen her staring out at the trees behind Elizabeth's house she'd seemed more shifter to him than human. Gage would take her either way but he wanted to give her the choice.

If he could bring her wolf close to the surface, even if she couldn't shift, she would feel more complete. But Marissa wouldn't be easy to convince.

Marissa gave enough of herself to be intriguing yet held back, making her a challenge. She'd spent time with him every night so far—sharing her body with him—yet she'd insisted on returning to her sister's house to stay most of the time. She kept a distance between them and he wasn't sure how to push the issue without sending her running.

"It would be a mistake to let her go. Not only does she need a Pack to protect her, but you're in love with her." The last was said quietly, but, to Gage's ears, it might as well have been yelled.

Gage spun around, denial on the tip of his tongue, but stopped himself. There was no reason to lie to Logan or himself.

He felt the change in the house, in him. Elizabeth and Marissa had arrived. "They're here." The timing got him out of confessing that Logan was right. He actually felt disappointed that he hadn't agreed out loud.

Logan nodded. "So let's get started."

They greeted the two women outside the door. Marissa smiled up at him and Gage's heart swelled. He *was* in love with her. Even if it had only been almost a week, even if he hadn't told her yet. The wolf inside him had chosen her and the man couldn't have picked better.

"Hi," Marissa greeted, looking beautiful in her short summer dress.

"Hello." Gage leaned down and kissed her mouth.

The blush that stole over her face would have been cute if it didn't tell him what he already knew. She was okay with what they did in private, but publicly she still shied away.

"I...um..." She nervously shifted from foot to foot. "Thanks for doing this."

Gage nodded and hugged her to his side. "You can thank me later," he whispered into her ear.

She gasped, and Elizabeth and Logan laughed out loud.

"Most of the guests have arrived and Greg is already outside," Logan, ever the peacemaker, announced.

The look of relief that crossed Marissa's face was comical. "She's ready," she responded, avoiding everyone's eyes.

Gage laughed, letting go of Marissa. He knew he shouldn't

tease her in front of others, but now that he had admitted to himself that he was in love with her, he wanted to shout it from the rooftops.

First, though, he had a ceremony to perform. He released Marissa but she didn't move away. That made him feel better. He gave her a wink before giving his attention to her sister.

"You look beautiful. Greg is very lucky," he told Elizabeth, kissing the top of her head.

"No. No. I'm the lucky one. I know that. He has been so patient with me for all these years." Elizabeth took a deep breath. "I love him."

"I know you do, honey. And it's time to do this." Marissa hugged her sister. She turned to Gage and offered him a smile as well.

Gage resisted the urge to kiss her once again. If he let himself, he would get all wrapped up with her and the ceremony wouldn't get started.

Logan offered Marissa his arm. "Allow me to take you to your seat, my lady."

Shyly, Marissa put her arm through Logan's. She liked him. He'd never treated her differently even after the embarrassing scene in the woods. Or for her relationship with Gage.

In fact, every time that Logan spoke with her he always brought up how great Gage was. Like he actually wanted to see them together. Marissa shook her head to let her thoughts go. This was Elizabeth's time and she needed to forget about the Alpha for a little bit.

Logan led her out of the back door to where the ceremony would take place. Gage would follow when it was time for the ceremony, escorting Elizabeth. As they headed to where the chairs had been set up, Marissa looked around, taking in the full picture. White lace and ribbons had been hung up. Her sister and Greg would stand under the arch while Gage performed the ceremony.

Lighthearted, Marissa smiled at the guests and Logan escorted her to the front. She didn't know the Pack and they only knew her as Elizabeth's sister. They wouldn't know she was defective.

She felt the unsettling sensation of eyes on her before understanding who was staring at her. Turning her head, she met the pair of dark brown eyes, eyes she knew so well. Eyes that had haunted her dreams for more years than she wanted to remember.

Almost stumbling in surprise, she was glad Logan was there.

"What's wrong?" he whispered.

"Nothing," she lied.

He would know it was a lie. Not only would he be able to smell it, but also she had started to tremble. She didn't know what Brandon was doing there but it couldn't be good. She watched Logan look over also and knew she wouldn't have a choice about telling Gage.

"Who is he?"

Tearing her gaze from Brandon's, Marissa held onto Logan. "My old Alpha's son," she whispered.

Logan knew little about what she'd been through and her relationship with Brandon was something she had shared only with Gage.

Oh, God, Gage was not going to be happy. He'd asked her repeatedly if she wanted him to look into her old Pack's action but Marissa didn't want any more trouble. It was time to let her past go and move on knowing she hadn't done anything wrong.

Logan got her to their seats in the front row. He would sit next to her for the ceremony — that had already been decided. She was now grateful for the arrangement as she could feel the other man's eyes on them as they sat.

Her palms were sweating and she rubbed her hands over the skirt of her dress. *Deep breaths*, that was all she needed to do. Ignore everyone but Elizabeth and Greg.

The music started, announcing Gage and Elizabeth, and

Logan placed his arm around the back of Marissa's chair. Protected, that was what she felt. Logan wasn't hitting on her. Instead, he was keeping her safe. She tried to relax, concentrating on her sister.

The ceremony was beautiful, and watching her sister commit to Greg brought tears to Marissa's eyes. It also served to take her attention away from the other guests. She watched Gage as he stood with pride and presented Greg and Elizabeth to the Pack and guests.

Their eyes met, causing a shiver of excitement to ripple through her entire body. He was like no other man she'd ever met. While he was domineering and demanding, he still remained calm and kind. She would never have thought that all the traits he carried could be found in one man, a wolf, and a Pack Alpha.

Logan nudged her, reminding her it was time to stand and walk to the reception. Marissa purposely kept her gaze straight ahead, avoiding any guests. She didn't know why Brandon was here and she should have no fear from him now, but years were hard to just replace. The promises and threats he'd made were still fresh in her mind.

Logan led Marissa to her sister, and while they hugged, he motioned for Gage to step aside. Marissa held Elizabeth, then Greg took her in his arms and kissed the top of her head. It felt brotherly and warm.

"I always wanted a sister. My mother had eight boys."

Laughing through happy tears, Marissa tilted her head back. "Well, you've got one now. You have no idea what you're in for." It had only been her and Elizabeth for so long that Marissa hoped Greg really meant his words.

Also laughing, Greg kissed her cheek. "I'll hold you to that, Marissa."

Marissa understood the warning. She wasn't done with this Pack. Greg considered her family and wouldn't let her disappear out of his and Elizabeth's lives.

An older couple walked up and Marissa was introduced to Greg's parents. They were sweet and loving and before she knew what was happening she was nodding as Greg's mom talked about the holidays. Marissa had no idea if she would be returning for them but the plans sure seemed good to her.

Elizabeth caught her hand and gave her a squeeze before leaning against her new mate. Marissa pulled out her phone so that she could capture the moment. They were beautiful together.

"What is it?" Gage asked, never taking his eyes off Marissa as he saw tears sparkle in her eyes. He knew she was thrilled for her sister, but he just wanted to hold her. Just be close to her as some of the Pack began to come up to the newly mated couple.

"I believe we have an unwanted guest." Logan kept his voice low so only his Alpha would hear.

Gage watched Greg kiss Marissa's cheek in a brotherly gesture. "Who?" he asked, distracted.

"Marissa's ex. The Alpha's son."

Shock had him giving his full attention to Logan. "Where? What did she say?" Gage had shared more with Logan than even Marissa knew. He trusted Logan with his life and in order to protect Marissa his second needed to be fully aware of the situation. He glanced around the yard, trying to spot the guy.

"She was upset, although she tried to hide it," Logan told him. "He didn't approach her but I could feel his gaze on us. It wasn't a good feeling."

"Find out what he's doing here," Gage ordered.

They didn't need this trouble. Marissa deserved to have this day with her sister. It was hard but Gage was able to push down his wolf instincts that wanted to attack and protect.

This was the shifter that had hurt the woman he loved. If Gage hadn't been an Alpha he didn't know if he would have had enough control to stop himself from making a scene.

As he glanced about he saw his guards in position around the gathering. He always made sure that his strongest wolves were on duty during any big event.

They were a large Pack and he had to ensure that they were safe. When the entire Pack got together teenagers acted out, children could wander off, and some wolves drank too much. Gage wouldn't take the chance of one of his Pack getting hurt.

He was never happier than at the moment that he took those precautions.

"I'll find out," Logan said. "But you should get over there."

Gage nodded and turned back toward the happy couple and Marissa. A man placed his hand on Marissa's back.

Gage didn't hold in his growl and he stomped forward. Marissa stiffened then turned and stepped out of his reach. "Brandon," she greeted but her eyes remained cold.

"You look beautiful, Marissa." He placed a kiss on her cheek before he turned and shook hands with Greg. "Congratulations."

"Thank you." Greg glanced between the new man and Marissa, knowing, Gage was sure, that something wasn't right but was unsure what to do.

"Congratulations, little wolf." Brandon also kissed Elizabeth's cheek.

"Thank you." Elizabeth's voice was soft. She sent her sister a panicked look. "Wh-what are you doing here, Brandon?"

"I escorted my cousin."

Gage had seen enough. He moved in beside Marissa.

"Gage." Her eyes pleaded with him as he stepped up to the small group.

She didn't want a scene, Gage recognized that. He was also the Alpha, and if anything happened his Pack would step in and that would be a mess. His wolves would follow his lead and they didn't need a riot.

The man turned to him. "Alpha." He nodded in respect. "That was a wonderful ceremony. One of the best I've ever witnessed."

Gage smiled and nodded back, running his hand over Marissa's back then settling his arm around her waist.

She flushed but didn't move away from him. Brandon's eyes narrowed slightly. Gage didn't smile but he wanted to.

"Uh... Gage, this is Brandon. He is the son of the Pack Alpha where we grew up." Marissa shifted like she wanted to move away from him, but Gage tightened his grip.

"Nice to meet you." Gage didn't move.

"Actually, I am now the Pack Alpha of the territory. My father has retired," Brandon said, keeping his eyes on her.

Gage kept calm. That announcement changed things. If Brandon was a Pack Alpha, he couldn't challenge Gage without permission from the Council that policed the Packs. Unless Brandon attacked his Pack directly, Gage's hands were tied. And Marissa wasn't part of his Pack. Damn, this was just getting more and more complicated.

"Congratulations, then," Gage told him with no feeling.

Marissa looked from one man to the other. Gage knew she was almost desperate to get away from Brandon. They would have to talk about what had happened between the two later, but right now his main objective was to help her out of her distress.

"They're starting the reception. We should take our seats," Gage told her, sliding his hand to hers. "If you'll excuse us," he said to Brandon but didn't wait for a response.

He walked away, taking Marissa with him while Greg and Elizabeth followed.

"I get the feeling I missed something," Greg murmured to his mate, but Gage heard him.

"That man is responsible for almost every problem we had in our old Pack." Elizabeth's voice held more bitterness than Gage had ever heard from her.

Marissa shrugged a shoulder and tried to pull away from Gage. He didn't release her. He could still feel the other man's gaze on them. He prayed that she would just give in this once. It wasn't easy for her and he understood that, but Gage was staking his claim. She was also still trembling slightly.

"It's going to be okay," he murmured to her as they reached their table.

He pulled out her chair and she looked at him.

"I don't want anything to ruin this day," she whispered. "Please."

Gage lifted his hand and brushed her bangs from her face. "I won't let anything happen. Not to upset Elizabeth or hurt you. I promise."

Marissa nodded. "Thank you."

She sat and Gage moved immediately to sit beside her, relieved when Logan filled the spare chair on the other side.

Seated between Gage and Logan, Marissa was safe enough for now. She'd tugged her hand away when she'd sat and he wanted to claim her once again, but he didn't press the issue. She had enough to deal with at the moment.

He glanced around. Brandon wasn't too far from them. The other Alpha's eyes were still on Marissa.

He was hanging on by a thin shred of control. His heart raced and his blood boiled in anger toward Brandon for everything Marissa had been through. Plus, suspicion as to what he was even doing here.

He peered over at Logan and could see the same feelings were going through his second. Whether Marissa was part of the Pack or not, she belonged to Gage.

He had never been so close to turning because of loss of control in front of any members of his Pack. He glanced around and nodded at the Pack Enforcers. It was their job to protect their Alpha. Each one was keeping a close eye on their leader, sensing something was not right. Gage was warning them to be on alert.

Marissa scooted her chair closer to him. Under the table, she placed her hand on his knee. "Look at me, Gage," she whispered.

He did and she smiled.

"I'm okay. Please don't start anything."

Not caring who was watching, Gage framed her face with both hands. "I won't if he doesn't."

Marissa dropped her gaze. "Please, Gage."

She wasn't comfortable with public displays. He understood that even if he didn't like it. He dropped his hands from her face. "He's not to get near you alone. Do you understand?"

Marissa nodded.

"Marissa." His voice was a low growl. He needed her to say the words.

"I understand," she told him quietly.

"Make sure, Marissa. You have no idea of the consequences," he warned.

"I promise, Gage."

With that, he relaxed next to her. What would happen was going to depend on Brandon. Gage was Alpha of this territory and he had a lot of Pack to protect. He wouldn't let an insult go. He had to prove he was strong. And he was. Brandon might have been named Alpha but Gage doubted that he'd earned the title.

Gage, on the other hand, had been trained since birth to take over for his father. His time in the military had given him the leadership skills that couldn't be taught. With one of the largest territories to protect, Gage kept up with all the exercises and fighting he could.

He even depended on some of his friends from other Packs to help him maintain the safety and care of his Pack. One of the scariest Enforcers in the country was Gage's best friend. Cain visited often and they always trained in both human and shifted form. Brandon might be an Alpha but his body was soft and he didn't have the same power that Gage knew radiated off him.

Brandon was untrained and untested. Gage was just looking for a reason to put the pup in his place.

Chapter Six

Marissa intended to keep her promise. She didn't want trouble for anyone and this was most definitely not the time or place. She didn't know why Brandon would even come to Elizabeth's mating ceremony, but he couldn't touch them. She told herself that over and over again. She was safe.

The seating placed her with Gage and Logan while members of her and Elizabeth's old Pack took up two tables across the yard. The other tables were filled with Gage's Pack. Everyone was behaving properly, but one wrong move from either Alpha could spell disaster. Wolves were territorial about almost everything, but particularly about their women.

Gage or Logan stayed with her the entire time. After pictures had been taken, dinner served and cake cut, the dancing began. Marissa danced with Gage, then Logan, but her attention was never too far from the man in the back keeping his eyes on her.

She knew Gage and Logan remained just as aware of him. Gage was trying to keep Marissa from looking over, but since he was just as guilty of looking she wasn't too worried.

Walking to get a refill of champagne, she stopped to talk to a few of the females from Gage's Pack who had openly befriended her. Elizabeth had some great friends. Logan was talking to two of the Enforcers, but kept an eye on her from a short distance.

Marissa received her refill then turned from the table, running into Brandon. She tried to step around him, but he moved also. She searched for Gage or Logan, but they were several feet away from her, involved in conversations.

Sighing, Marissa pulled her shoulders back and met Brandon's gaze. "What do you want?" she snapped. She had no reason to be polite. The night was ending and she would never see him again.

He had tormented her enough and Marissa was angry, and having him in front of her was bringing it all to the surface. The anger was burning away the fear she'd felt just thinking about him. She was tired of being afraid.

Brandon stepped toward her. "Interesting seeing you interact with another Pack."

Marissa dropped her eyes out of habit, her confidence leaving her as he spoke with authority. She'd never heard that tone before.

Guess he really is an Alpha.

Although he had nowhere near the power that Gage had.

Seeming satisfied, he moved even closer. "We have a lot to talk about."

"We have nothing to talk about," she said to her feet.

"Oh, you are very wrong. As Alpha of the Pack, I now have access to all the data on you and your family," Brandon said.

"So?" Marissa asked. Why would he need that? Why would he even care?

"So as your Pack Alpha—"

"You are *not* my Pack Alpha," she interrupted. How dare he.

Lifting his hand, he brushed her hair off her face. "Actually I am."

Marissa shook. This couldn't be happening. "I was kicked out of the Pack. You have no power over me."

"Well, funny thing about that. My father never turned in your papers to the Council to let them know you were leaving the Pack. As law states, a member cannot leave the Pack and go rogue without a trial or the proper paperwork. You still belong to the Pack. To me."

"No." Marissa stepped back, shaking her head.

No, no, no.

She wouldn't go back to his Pack. She'd die before ever returning to him and giving him power over her once again. It had almost killed her the last time he'd used her. Marissa could look back and see that their relationship had been nothing more than a spoiled bratty shifter wanting to piss off his daddy by banging the Pack joke. It hurt to have to admit that Brandon hadn't loved her the way she had him.

When she'd first been chased from her home, Marissa had been sure that Brandon would come after her. It'd only taken weeks for her to realize that Brandon had no intention of going up against his father to claim her the way he'd always promised he would.

"That can't be right," she murmured, more to herself than him.

Brandon laughed. "Yes, it's true. And by Wolf law, I have full control over you for your safety and wellbeing."

"You don't know anything about laws. You are a liar just like your father."

Anger flashed in his eyes and Marissa felt true fear. Her throat went dry while her heart pounded. Reaching out, he grabbed her arm. It hurt and she knew his touch would leave a bruise. Marissa frantically looked around for Gage or Logan, not seeing either.

"No one's going to come to your rescue this time." He yanked her to him.

His breath fanned against her cheek. She clenched her eyes closed. How? How had such an awesome event led to this? She'd just wanted to watch her sister and dance with Gage.

"And be careful of your words. I will not let you disrespect my father."

"Let me go!" Marissa desperately tried to pull away from him, the need to run and hide almost overbearing.

"Or what?" Brandon ran his cheek over her hair. "You are mine. And you will be coming back to the territory with me."

Tears filled Marissa's eyes. This wasn't happening. This couldn't be. "No."

"What? Don't want to leave your lovers?" he spat at her. "Just how many of the wolves here have you spread your legs for?"

Marissa shook her head and again tried to pull away.

"I already know you are fucking the Alpha and his Beta. Is it just those two or did you take them all?"

As he shook her, Marissa's head snapped back painfully. She heard a growl before she was knocked away from him. Peering up from where she'd fallen, she saw a blur of movement as two males went down on the ground.

It took a moment for Marissa to recognize the man fighting with Brandon as one of Gage's guards, not Gage. That was both good and bad. If Gage had attacked Brandon there would be hell to pay. But she didn't want to see this poor guard get in trouble when he had saved her.

"Stop!" she yelled to the two men.

They didn't hear her...or chose to ignore her.

It wasn't until there was a second growl and Gage ordered, "Stop," that all movement ceased around her.

Marissa peeked up to see his furious eyes boring into her. The muscle in his cheek jumped as he clenched his teeth. Marissa immediately dropped her gaze. This was all her fault. She couldn't control herself, Brandon, or anyone else.

"Sam, go to my office," he told his guard, keeping his voice even, not giving away what he was thinking.

Sam picked himself up off the ground, looking one last time at the man he'd taken down. "Yes, Alpha."

"Marissa, come here," he ordered next.

Marissa moved quickly to obey. It would not be good to leave Gage waiting when every single person had their full attention on him. Wrapping his hand around her wrist, Gage held her next to him. She leaned against him, relieved that it was him touching her. She didn't think she'd ever be able to pull away from him again after having Brandon's hands on her. Logan stepped into the middle of the group and nodded at his Alpha.

"I believe our guests have overstayed their welcome. Now that the happy couple has left, they shall be escorted out." Gage's voice was low and deadly. Daring anyone to challenge him.

"I'll see to it, Alpha." Logan nodded and reached for Brandon, who pushed his hands away.

Standing on his own, Brandon faced off with Gage. "I agree we should be leaving. We'll just be taking Marissa with us," he said smugly.

Marissa stepped behind Gage, using him as a shield. She wasn't going with Brandon. She didn't think Gage would make her, but, if what Brandon had said were true, he might not have a choice.

"I don't think so." Gage didn't sound amused as Brandon stood in front of him.

Brandon smiled. "As her Pack Alpha, I will be returning her home."

"Pack Alpha?" Gage looked over his shoulder at her. Marissa shook her head. He faced Brandon again. "I think not."

"She was born into my Pack."

"And left your Pack at the request of your Alpha."

"Really?" Brandon challenged, crossing his arms over his chest. "I have no paperwork supporting that."

"Of course not." Gage nodded as if he understood.

Marissa panicked. "Gage."

"Hush," he ordered. She fell silent. "Well, then I suppose you have the paperwork stating that she does belong to your Pack."

The smile faded on Brandon's face. "I do. Not with me, though."

Gage shook his head. "I cannot in good conscience turn over a female who I don't know truly belongs with you."

Brandon took one step forward. "You would start a war over this slut?"

Marissa gripped the back of Gage's shirt. She didn't think Gage would turn her over to the other man, but doubt still made her stomach tighten with nerves.

Gage didn't move but met the other Alpha's stare. "Would *you*? You are in my territory now."

Brandon relaxed his stance. "We'll see about this." He turned and walked away, his Pack members following him.

"Make sure they all leave, Logan. Then I want you in my office."

Logan nodded first to his Alpha then to the other Enforcers who had surrounded them. They all left silently.

After turning, Gage grabbed Marissa's arm and pulled her toward the house.

"Party's over," he threw back over his shoulder at the other members of his Pack, having them disperse quickly.

Marissa remained quiet as Gage led her away. In the shoes she wore, she kept tripping. Gage didn't slow his steps. However, he did tighten his hold. Even though he was really towing her along and his hold was strong, it didn't hurt. Because Gage wouldn't hurt her. Not physically. But if he gave her over to Brandon, it would break her.

Sam jumped up when Gage walked into his office with Marissa. Gage pointed to the couch and waited for Marissa to sit before turning to his Enforcer.

"I apologize for my action, Alpha. I have no excuse for starting a fight with another wolf without your permission."

Gage nodded. "Yes. Especially another Alpha."

Sam's eyes widened. He hadn't known that Brandon was an Alpha. If his guard couldn't detect the power, Gage knew he'd been correct about Brandon not carrying the authority needed to lead. That was valuable information.

Sam wiped his dirty hands on his pants. "I can only say that I was protecting the woman that my Alpha has taken as his own. He had his hands on her and she was protesting."

"And for that I thank you. Stand down, Sam, you are not in trouble."

Sam relaxed. He glanced from Marissa back to him. "Is everything okay?"

Gage shook his head and walked behind his desk. "I don't know. But I have a favor to ask."

"Anything, Alpha," Sam agreed without second thought.

"We have a problem with the other Pack. Marissa will be staying here at the main house. I would like for you to go to Elizabeth's house and bring Marissa's belongings here."

Marissa opened her mouth then closed it quickly.

"Then we are on high alert. I want a full watch. Especially around the house."

Sam nodded. Logan knocked and entered the office. Gage acknowledged him with a tilt of his head.

"Then I would like you to stay here at the house with Logan and me, in case there is any trouble."

"Of course, Alpha."

Gage dismissed Sam and turned to Logan.

"They're gone. The gate is closed and locked. I have four men on guard there," Logan informed him.

"Good. Make sure Sam has the others doing rounds," Gage told him, even though he knew Logan would take all the precautions that were needed. Still, he felt better knowing everything would be in order to protect Marissa.

"Yes, Alpha. No one will get in without permission."

Gage wanted more security than that. "I want no one else leaving." He wouldn't put it past Brandon to take someone from his Pack to try to trade for Marissa. "Also call Greg and warn him. Preferably without Elizabeth knowing. I want them to enjoy their honeymoon but also be careful."

"I'll make sure of it," Logan promised and Gage knew he would be taking care of things personally. "Anything else, Alpha?"

Gage looked over at Marissa. She had been silent the entire time. "Get me what you can, Logan. I want these files that he's talking about. Also anything on the Alpha position transfer. I want what was sent to the Council. Call my father if you have to."

"I'll get started right away." Logan glanced at Marissa before he nodded and silently left the office.

Gage stalked to Marissa and wasn't surprised when she leaned away from him. He'd done his duty to make sure his Pack was safe and now was the time for comfort.

"Come here," he said.

Slowly Marissa stood and took his hand, keeping her eyes down at her feet. Gage gently led her from his office and up the stairs. Once they reached his bedroom, he let her enter first. Marissa walked into the large room then sat on the edge of the bed.

Dropping to his knees in front of her, Gage gripped her hands. "Talk to me," he demanded softly.

Marissa didn't hold back her tears any longer. "I'm sorry, Gage! I'm so sorry."

Getting up and sitting next to her, he wrapped his arms around her. It broke his heart to see her so upset. "Shh."

"I… I…don't know what to do!"

Gage held her close to him and tried to make her feel protected. "I'll take care of it. Take care of you," he promised her and meant every word. She would never have to go through that again. She belonged to him now and Gage would spend the rest of his life showing her how loved and wanted she was. No one would ever put their hands on her again.

He was so pissed off at himself for letting it happen in the first place. He'd thought that Logan was with her when he'd allowed one of his Pack members to engage him in a conversation. He should have kept a better eye on her. "It's going to be okay."

"He'll start a war. I don't know why. But I know he will," she managed to get out between sobs.

"Shh. Baby, let him try," Gage said as he stroked her back.

"I don't want anyone hurt because of me. I don't understand why he's doing this."

Picking her up, Gage then took her to the head of the bed and pulled the covers back. He placed her gently down.

"Please don't worry, Marissa. I will take care of this."

Tears still streaked her face. "I won't go with him."

"I know, baby. I wouldn't let you even if you wanted to." He allowed her to wear herself out with the tears and sobbing. Gage hoped that would help her clear her mind and let go of her fear. It went on for several minutes before she quieted.

Gage wiped the tears from her face before bending down and kissing her cheeks, nose, eyes and forehead then placing a light one on her lips.

"Sleep now. I'll be here when you wake." Gage waited until her eyes closed. He stood and thought about what to do next.

* * * *

Gage stood from where he sat at the table in his room. True to his word, he'd worked up here instead of his office. Marissa was still deep asleep as if she couldn't handle any more stress. He wanted to take her away from all this but he knew that the best way to protect her was breaking any bonds that still remained with her old Pack.

He'd studied the papers he'd gotten when he'd first looked into Marissa. Logan and Sam were in his office trying to find something else—anything else. Brandon had been correct that the proper paperwork for Marissa's dismissal from her birth Pack had never been filed. That was a problem.

Luckily Gage had resources.

A phone call to another Alpha—Lamont from three territories away—had helped. He had even offered to send Cain, his son—who was also the same man Gage had been thinking about earlier—down if Gage needed any help.

Grateful to have the older Alpha behind him, Gage relaxed. As Lamont had stated, there had always been something wrong with Marissa's original Pack. And while they would probably find papers to claim Marissa as theirs,

Gage could turn around and file a claim that Marissa had been thrown out and had not been protected by her Pack. Gage knew he had a good case for that. Marissa had been on her own for the past ten years.

It also meant that Gage would have to take her into his Pack to file those papers and keep her from Brandon. He didn't mind having her there. She'd be a good member, but he wanted more. He wanted a commitment from her. He'd found his life-mate. Marissa would be the obstacle that they'd have to overcome for that to happen.

The light knock on the door took his attention from his thoughts. Walking quietly to the door, he opened it to Hannah, one of the older females who helped with his house. She had worked for his father before him and had always been a surrogate mother to him.

"I brought you both some bread and soup. And made her some tea," she told him.

Gage opened the door wider to let her come in with the tray. She placed the tray on the clean side of the table before looking up at him. Hannah had been with the Pack for fifty years. She had come to his father after a member in her old Pack had assaulted her. Her Alpha hadn't done anything and Hannah had run away. Gage's father had gladly taken her into his Pack and his home. She had cooked for the wolves and kept his house ever since.

"You're doing a good thing," she said, tears in her eyes.

Gage shrugged. "I'm not only doing it for her."

"I know." She placed one hand on his cheek. "She wouldn't make it there. It would take everything out of her until she slowly died."

Gage placed his hand over hers, sharing comfort with her. "I will protect her. Even if it costs me my life."

"I know." She smiled sadly. "And that is why I choose to follow you like I did your father." She left him with that.

Gage walked over to Marissa. She was curled up and had dried tears on her face. Running his fingers over her cheek, he watched her blink awake.

"Hi," he greeted once her eyes opened.

She blushed and looked away. "Hi."

Leaning over her, he took her lips. Marissa opened for him, wrapping her arms around his neck. Gage moaned into the kiss and pressed her back into the bed. The power and control she held shimmered beneath the surface. She pulled at his shirt, finally getting it over his head and her tongue on his chest. The muscles under her mouth quivered and his breath brushed against her cheek.

Gage used his lips on her shoulders, then pulled the straps of her dress down her arms. She still wore the dress from the ceremony and he wanted it off her. Reaching behind her, he unzipped it, baring her to him.

The rest of the clothes were quickly removed while they touched and kissed each other's skin. When he positioned himself over her, he held her legs open with his own. He entered her slowly, as they watched each other.

Being together like this always made Gage feel complete. He didn't understand how Marissa could push him away after they'd made love.

Marissa lifted her hips up to allow Gage to slip in smoothly all the way. He filled her, and she started to move under him. Gage kept his strokes slow and deep, watching the emotions in her eyes as he brought her pleasure. Her mouth opened and small sounds came from her. Gage grunted, the natural pace picked up, his body demanding he take her, the wolf demanding he claim her.

The sounds of their flesh slapping together was loud in the quiet of the room and sounded erotic. Her pussy was tight and her inner muscles tried to hold him in each time he withdrew. Gage thrust inside her faster and harder. He gripped her hips and lifted her up off the bed to change the angle and really slam into her.

He loved the fact that she not only took everything he had to offer but was begging him for more.

Crying out, Marissa wrapped her legs higher around his waist, taking him deeper. "Yes. Gage. Oh yes."

"Mine," he growled. "Mine."

"Yes." Marissa eyes glowed, showing the rare glimpse of her wolf. "Yes, Gage, take me."

Gage plunged into her over and over. "More. I want more."

"Yes," she cried out. "Anything!"

"Tell me you're mine. Mine."

"Yes. I'm yours. Take me Gage. Claim me." The words came out, flowing from her without hesitation.

That was all Gage needed to hear. He pulled out and turned her over. He placed her on all fours and entered her quickly, going all the way until she could feel his balls against her thighs. His cock was buried deep and she was moaning while pushing herself back.

Gage thrust into her fast and hard, holding her hips and running his lips over her back. When he felt her body start to tremble and she cried out her release, he opened his mouth. His canines lengthened, and he bit down, sinking his teeth into her shoulder. Her blood flowed freely as he claimed her as his own.

He didn't need to swallow much of her blood. Just the exchange would link them. Gage lifted his head to stare down at the mark. His cock pulsed and he came.

Licking at the wound, he cleaned it as he found his own release, pulling her along with him one more time.

Empty and satisfied, he turned her back over and took her lips. He shared her blood with her, licking. He bit down on his tongue, filling his mouth with his own blood. He held the back of her head firmly as he forced his blood into her.

With the claiming and blood exchange finished, they collapsed as mates.

Chapter Seven

Gage held Marissa in his arms and caressed her body. She hadn't said anything since they'd finished the claiming, but she hadn't pulled away either. Her body remained relaxed and soft.

When she rubbed along him, he felt the wetness between her thighs—evidence of the claiming and mating still running through her body. Cupping her round bottom, he lifted her up and onto his thighs.

"Ride me, baby. Fuck me."

She did. She rode him fast, raising herself up and down, her clit rubbing against him while he played with her nipples.

"Mine." He lifted his mouth to take one pert nub inside.

Marissa cried out, riding him faster, taking them both to a quick but powerful climax. Sweating and panting, she fell on his chest.

Gage held her close. "I love you."

Marissa jerked and brought her head up. "What?"

Gage laughed at the expression on her face. With a hand in her hair, he brought her mouth inches from his. "You heard me."

"But—"

Gage nipped her lip. "I've claimed you. Why would I do that if I didn't love you?"

"To protect me. To keep me in your Pack."

Gage's stomach dropped. Was that what she really thought? Was that why she'd done it, allowed him to claim her? Gage started to pull her off him.

Marissa tightened her legs, holding Gage under her.

Inside her.

"Marissa."

Marissa just shook her head. "I'm sorry."

Gage sighed. He'd been stupid. Thinking she would fall in love as fast as he had. But he'd known the first time he'd seen her looking defiant and angry that she was the one who would take his heart. He'd known she wasn't ready but had let her words during passion override his senses.

Using his strength, he lifted her off of him. She growled but he ignored her and stood.

"Where are you going?" she asked.

He knew she was reaching for him but Gage really couldn't listen to her reject him. He'd put everything on the line and his heart was breaking.

Gage didn't even turn around. "To shower. We still have a lot to do to take care of your old Pack." He didn't raise his voice. It wasn't really her fault. No, this was all on him. He'd promised himself that he wouldn't push her but the minute he'd gotten lost in her body he'd done just that.

He'd demanded that she submit and accept him and she had. But why had he given in? Anger at himself had him striding across the room quickly.

Marissa watched his back as he stalked into the bathroom and slammed the door. Shit, that hadn't gone well. The wolf inside her complained and demanded she go after her mate.

She should have told him that she loved him too. And she did. The first time he'd kissed her, he had taken her heart along with her soul. He was everything to her, but giving him knowledge of that was hard for her. She'd only told one other man that she'd loved him and Brandon had used that confession against her.

Huffing out an irritated breath, Marissa stood and followed. She smiled when the knob turned in her hand and she opened the door. She could see Gage, through the glass, with both hands braced on the wall and his head bent under the spray. Pulling in all her courage, she opened the glass door and stepped silently behind him.

He jumped as she touched his back. "What are you doing?"

Marissa leaned into him, pressing her naked body to his. "Helping you shower." She reached over and picked up the soap from the dish.

Using shaking hands, afraid of rejection, she began washing his body. Running her soapy palms over his shoulders, down his strong back, to the sculpted ass she wanted to sink her teeth into, she took in his scent. Mixed with sweat, soap, and her own aroma.

It was hard to form the words that she wanted to give him but she could show him with her actions that she did love him. Needed and wanted him.

Kneeling behind him, she began to run her hands up and down his legs. She slipped her hands over his body and kneaded the flesh she washed.

When she caressed his cheeks then ran a finger between them, his body shivered. Marissa liked the reaction. Gage had introduced her to so much in the past week about what making love meant instead of fucking. Maybe, just maybe, she could do the same for him. To show him how she felt.

She wasn't a hundred percent sure what she was doing. Her hand worked on its own as she washed and touched him. She had her fingers between his legs, teasing over his anus before slipping forward to massage his sac.

She'd had sex with lots of guys but no one had ever reached her, meant anything, like Gage did. With her experience she knew how to please a man. They all liked different things and Marissa wanted to share everything with Gage. To find out what he enjoyed.

He shuddered at her touch and she moved with more confidence. While rubbing his sac then his thick cock, she used her other hand to brush over his tight hole. Slowly and carefully, she slipped just the tip of her finger carefully in and out.

His breath rushed out and he groaned. His hands on the shower wall started to shake. Marissa continued to stroke him with one hand while she pushed her finger into the back entrance that had never been penetrated. She knew he'd never had it done before — they'd talked about all their sexual experiences and likes.

Gage was tight but he wasn't stopping her. Marissa had done this before and if the man was comfortable with this kind of play they usually ended up coming harder than ever before.

His hips moved as she grew in confidence and fingered his prostate. A conversation about spanking and how much she liked it had made way to them opening up about all of their desires. He'd told her this was something he was willing to try with the right partner. And *she* was the right partner, the only one he would have from now on, and she was a mate who wouldn't share.

She matched her rhythm on his shaft to the strokes in and out of his ass, finally pushing her finger all the way inside. His hips moved forward, rubbing against her hands before slamming back on her finger. Gage picked up the speed with his movements and Marissa added a second finger. He groaned and she knew he was close to climax. The hoarse cry that tore out of his throat echoed around the bathroom as his body bucked and he started to spill his seed over Marissa's hand and the shower tile.

Once he'd released, Marissa took her hands from him and kissed her way up. When she reached his shoulder, she bit into it. Gage's body jerked under her. She slipped between him and the shower wall, then she met his eyes.

"I love you, Gage. I have from the beginning. And you are mine too."

Emotions broke out over his face, and he wrapped his arms around her as he kissed her all over her face.

Marissa felt perfectly at peace. The way she should after mating with him. This was it. She might have messed up earlier but she had made it up to him.

They ignored the light knock on the door. The knock came again, so he lifted his head and yelled. "Go away!"

The knock sounded again and she heard Logan's voice. "I apologize for interrupting, Alpha."

"Then don't," Gage complained, keeping contact with her.

Marissa nibbled at his jaw while she traced his cock with her fingers. If Logan would go away they could have another round before getting something substantial to eat.

"Yes, sir," Logan said. "I wouldn't be bothering you, except you have a visitor."

Gage's face shut down. He reached over and turned off the water. Grabbing a towel, he wrapped it around his waist while looking back at her with hot promise in his eyes. She could see the regret but understood. Gage was an Alpha and he had an entire Pack he needed to watch out for. As much as she wanted to lock him inside the room and keep him all to herself, she couldn't. He handed her a large towel and waited until she'd covered herself her before yanking the door open.

"And just who did you let in without my permission?" he asked Logan.

Logan grinned. "Your father, Alpha."

Marissa's heart sank. That couldn't be good news. Gage had told her that his father was one of the ex-Alphas on the Council. Since he was based in California, a surprise visit was probably bad news.

Gage laughed, confusing her. "I should have guessed. We'll be right down."

"Yes, Alpha." Logan stepped away from the door.

Gage beckoned for Marissa to leave the bathroom with him. He didn't say anything so she just followed his lead.

Gage pulled his clothes on quickly while watching her do the same. Marissa would have put on a show for him if they hadn't had his dad waiting somewhere in the house for them. Instead, she dressed as fast as she could.

"I hate to see you cover that beautiful body," Gage teased.

Yanking on her jeans, Marissa sent him a dirty look. "Well, I'm not meeting your father without clothes on."

Gage stalked toward her. "Okay, how about just without the panties?"

Marissa moved out of his reach. He could have caught her, but he was trying to relax her. It was obvious she was nervous about his father being there. "Come on! It's your house now too."

"Absolutely not! It's bad enough we both have wet hair so he'll probably guess what we were doing."

"Oh, he'll more than guess since we smell like each other and sex." Gage wrapped an arm around her waist as she tried to get her shirt on.

"Stop that," Marissa ordered, but he didn't miss the smile playing at the corner of her lips.

"Just lose the panties and I'll be good."

She shook her head. "I don't know what this obsession is with my underwear but you are one kinky wolf."

Gage laughed. "You have no idea." Fuck, his ass was still tingling from her earlier fingering. He'd thought about it before but hadn't been sure he'd like it. Growing up in the Pack where other shifters had no problem sharing their sex life had educated him at an early age. He had friends both straight and gay who loved anal play.

Marissa had proved she was into their sex just as much as him.

She bent over to pick up her flip-flops and he spanked her ass. Hard.

She squeaked before spinning around. "Gage!"

He winked. "Just warming you up for later."

She bit her lip as her face flushed. He easily picked up on her arousal. Oh yeah, they were going to have more fun.

He held out his hand. "Then let's go get this over with so we can get back to what we were doing."

Marissa put her hand in his and he towed her from the room.

"What's he doing here?" she asked. Nerves were obvious in her voice.

"He probably heard about the trouble. Logan called him earlier to see if your old Pack ever filed any papers releasing you from them."

"Oh," she whispered.

Gage tugged her to a stop and pushed her against the wall. He covered her body with his before pressing his forehead to hers. "You have nothing to worry about. My father will love you just as much as I do. As everyone who knows you does."

She took a deep breath. "Just don't leave me alone with him. I don't know how to deal with fathers unless they're assholes."

Gage laughed. "You got it."

He kissed her quickly then linked his fingers with hers and tugged her along.

They walked into the living room just as Logan handed Gage's father a glass filled with brown liquid.

"Father," Gage greeted.

He let go of Marissa's hand and she moved behind him. He wasn't really surprised.

His father stood and walked over quickly. "Son."

The two men stood for a moment before laughing and embracing in a big hug. The hold lasted several minutes before his dad turned his eyes to his mate.

She looked practically ready to run. Gage knew his father would understand and put her at ease. Even before any of this had happened, Gage had told his father about her.

"You must be Marissa."

Marissa nodded and dropped her eyes. Gage wanted to tell her that wasn't necessary, but his father moved first.

"My daughter," he said softly as he hugged her to him. "I welcome you into my family."

When he pulled away, Gage noticed the surprise on her face and knew his father hadn't missed it either.

"I am so pleased to meet my son's chosen."

Marissa glanced over at Gage, and he smiled at her reassuringly. She relaxed visibly and looked at his father.

"It is nice to meet you too." Her voice was soft but strong.

Showing her strength even when she was afraid. Gage was so proud.

His father took her arm and headed for the couch. Gage followed and sat in a chair across from them. Logan remained by the door, still on watch.

"We'll have plenty of time to get to know each other better, but first, let's discuss this situation with the other Pack," his father told Marissa as they sat.

She nodded even though she didn't look excited about the conversation.

Thirty minutes later, Marissa was arguing with both men.

"There should be no challenge!" Her voice rose above the rest.

Gage shook his head. "He will challenge me. And I have to accept." He knew she didn't want him to, but she had to understand where he was coming from. Protecting her was his duty. As an Alpha he couldn't refuse.

"You don't have to do anything," she argued.

"He must protect his mate." His father spoke the words Gage had been thinking.

Frustrated, Marissa stomped to the window and peered out.

Gage followed her.

"I don't want anyone getting hurt because of me," she said more quietly.

Gage wrapped his arms around her and rested his chin on the top of her head.

"Baby, even if we weren't mated, which we are, I would accept a challenge from him for everything he put you and your sister through." He turned her around so he could see her eyes. "I love you. I will make sure you are always protected."

Reaching up, Marissa cupped his cheeks. "I love you."

As their lips met in a soft kiss, all of their troubles seemed to melt away. The kiss went deeper, and someone cleared their throat from across the room. Gage and Marissa broke away, but Gage held onto her.

"Sorry," she mumbled, embarrassed.

Gage's father's eyes were bright with unshed tears. "It's understandable. I can remember—" His cell phone ringing cut him off. He shrugged before he answered.

The conversation was brief. Gage could hear what was being said on both sides of the phone. He relaxed and hoped that Marissa could feel the tension drain from him. When the phone call was over, Gage hugged her tightly.

"There will be no challenge," Gage's father announced.

Marissa jerked in his arms. "Really?"

Gage's dad nodded. "Seems Brandon's father stepped in and won't allow him to take this any further." He looked at Gage. "Even retired, he still has some control over his son, it seems."

"Oh, thank God!" Marissa kissed Gage quickly. He tried to return it but his mind was whirling. This was too easy. While Gage believed that Brandon's dad still controlled him, he'd also seen the look on Brandon's face when he'd watched Marissa. Brandon wanted Gage's mate and Gage was finding it hard to imagine that he would just give her up.

Gage wouldn't. Nothing and no one could get Marissa away from him.

"What's wrong?" she asked when he didn't say anything.

Gage smiled and kissed her back. "Nothing, baby. This is good. Why don't you go upstairs and change, and we'll take my father to town for a steak dinner?" He needed a minute to talk to his father and Logan.

Marissa nodded even while she peered suspiciously at him. He knew she would still worry, but he didn't want her involved in the next discussion. She glanced over her shoulder then opened the door and he sent her what he hoped was a relaxed smile.

Gage waited until he heard the bedroom door open before

speaking. He looked at his father then his Beta.

"This isn't over. No matter what they say, they are up to something," Gage said.

Logan took a few steps from his post by the door. "I saw his face when he said Marissa belonged with him. It doesn't matter what his father told him," Logan added.

Gage's father rubbed a hand over his face. "I agree with both of you. And since he is Alpha now, he doesn't have to follow what his father says."

Gage thought of when Marissa had told him that she loved him. He hadn't cared about the other Pack. He'd only cared about having her in his arms for the rest of his life. He wasn't about to give that up.

"From everything I've read and what Marissa's told me, I don't think he'll come at me through proper channels."

"An ambush, maybe?" Logan suggested.

"Or they may just try to take her," Gage's dad mused.

"They won't get her," Gage assured the men. "They would have to get through me first."

His dad nodded, but worry was etched on his face. "That doesn't mean that they won't try. You need to get more guards. Call in for some help. Brandon will try to kill you if he can and he won't do it alone."

"Let them try. I would love a chance to go after that entire Pack for what they did to Marissa." He fisted his hands in anger just thinking about what his mate had gone through. He slowly unclenched them and ran a frustrated hand over his face.

"You need to keep a calm head," his father advised, walking over to refill his glass.

"And what would you do?" Getting angry, Gage began to pace the room. He'd earned his rank as Alpha and he wasn't going to let some still-wet-behind-the-ears pup challenge him. Marissa would not live in fear for the rest of her life.

His father took his time refilling his drink and sipping before responding. "I'm no longer the Alpha of the Pack, so it doesn't matter. What does is how you handle this threat to *your* Pack."

Gage nodded. His father had always run the Pack fairly, and they'd thrived under his leadership. "I understand I can't go looking for trouble. But if they bring it to me, I will be ready for them. The only way they'll get to her is to come into my territory."

Logan cleared his throat and drew both men's attention. "So she's not leaving?"

"Of course not!" Gage shouted.

Logan nodded and dropped his eyes in a submissive gesture.

"Damn! I'm sorry, Logan. I didn't mean to take it out on you," Gage said sincerely. There was no reason to get angry at his best friend.

"It's okay." Logan grinned at him. "I would be worried if you weren't on edge."

His father walked over then threw his arm around Gage's shoulder. "I think I'll take a rain check on dinner. Logan can keep me company. You need to go see your mate. Calm down and spend some quality time with her."

Gage went without looking at either man. Who would have thought falling in love and claiming a mate would make him feel so out of control? His dad was right—he needed to bond with Marissa. That would calm both him and his wolf down.

He reached the bedroom door and opened it quietly. Marissa sat on the bed with her hands in her lap.

"Are you done discussing whatever you didn't want me to hear?" she asked.

Gage sighed as he closed the door before he leaned against it. "How much did you listen to?"

"None of it," she admitted. "But I can read you, Gage. You wanted to talk to your dad and Logan alone."

"You're right," he admitted. He wouldn't lie to her. That was not the way he wanted their relationship to start.

"So what's going on?" she questioned while she stood.

"I think that Brandon is still coming after you," he said.

"No." Marissa shook her head. "His dad told him to stay away."

Gage cupped her face. "He wants you and I find it difficult to believe that just a word from his dad will stop you. What do you think?"

Marissa's opinion was going to be the most helpful. She had known Brandon for a long time.

"I wish I knew," she said. "But I can honestly say that I never expected to see him again. After I was kicked out of the Pack I waited around town for weeks but he never came and found me."

Gage nodded for her to continue.

"I've been on my own for over ten years, why now?" she said.

That was a very good question. If Brandon hadn't been looking for her, why'd he just shown up now?

"Can we just…" Marissa waved her hand around.

He knew what she needed. Gage pulled her toward the bed. "Yeah we can."

Chapter Eight

"Would you like to repeat that?" Marissa asked even though she was certain she'd heard Gage correctly.

"You need to make arrangements to have your stuff sent here," he told her.

He was currently prowling the bedroom floor, looking very much on the edge. He had been sweet and loving last night, and that morning when he'd woken her in the most pleasurable way. Now, fifteen minutes later, he was issuing orders. Marissa's head spun from his abrupt change of attitude.

"My stuff?" Marissa kept herself calm, knowing one of them had to be. "I think we need to discuss this."

"What's to discuss? You are my mate. I can't leave my Pack or my territory, so you have to move here," he announced, staring at her like it didn't even need to be said.

Marissa took in his demeanor and knew this could turn bad real fast. "Gage. I don't know that I want to live in Pack territory."

She saw the change in him immediately. His eyes went flat and cold, and his face hardened.

"You don't have a choice."

"I… I don't have a choice?" Her voice rose. She was just as close to losing control. She was trying, really trying to remain calm but she didn't give in to orders.

"That's what I said. *You are my mate,*" he yelled.

"I may be your mate, but I don't belong to you, Gage Wolf," she yelled back. Forget being calm. She wasn't going to let him dictate to her about her future. If they couldn't discuss this like adults, maybe a good fight would do them both good.

"Actually, that is *exactly* what that means," Gage hollered.

Marissa stood toe to toe with him. Even with anger burning in his eyes she didn't fear him. "I have a life in California."

"You have a life here with me where you'll be safe," Gage said. "I can't allow you to leave until we *know* you're safe."

"Allow me?" Marissa repeated. "You're actually going to stand there and go Alpha on me."

He barked out a laugh. "In case you forgot, I am your Alpha."

"Oh, how could I forget?" she snapped. "You're sure acting like an Alpha asshole."

Gage growled. "Don't you dare," he warned.

"What are you going to do?" she taunted. "Tie me to the bed?"

Gage smiled. "That's not a bad idea." He calmed down and was growing aroused.

"Ugh!" she screamed in frustration.

He started a fight then wanted to jump right back into bed?

"Damn it, Marissa," Gage said at normal level before he walked over and dropped onto the bed. "I'm just trying to keep you safe."

"I've been keeping myself safe for a lot of years," she told him.

"I know," Gage said. "But it's my job now."

"No." She pointed her finger at him. "You won't dictate how I live my life."

"Yes I will," he snapped back. "And you are going to listen to me on this."

Marissa twitched in surprise. She knew that he was dominant but he'd never made her feel like she wasn't equal until that moment.

Gage watched as Marissa's face fell and she jerked as if he'd just struck her. Damn, this was not going the way he wanted. He hadn't meant to bring it up at all, but he just wanted her safe in his home, in his arms.

"I didn't mean it like that," he said and took deep breaths to relax himself. His emotions were too high and he was making a mess of things.

She turned away from him and he had to stop himself from reaching for her. Give her the space she needed.

"I think it is what you meant, Gage. You may not be like my old Pack leader, but you are an Alpha."

"I am in no way like your last Pack leader. This Pack is nothing like your old one. The sooner you realize that, the better off you will be."

"Maybe," she said softly, turning back toward him. "But how long until you start giving me orders every day? I have to be in an equal relationship." She took a deep breath. "I'll admit that I like it when you dominate me in bed. Hell, I more than like it. But it can't be like that all the time."

He could see unshed tears and it broke his heart that he'd hurt her. "Baby, I'm sorry…"

She held up a hand to stop him from approaching. "I know I have issues, Gage. You knew that coming into this. I can't just forget everything in my past. And you can't expect me to drop my entire life."

He knew what she was saying and she was right but they were mates. "You actually think that you can just walk away from me, from your mate? Marissa, think about this." He had to make her see reason.

"I am. What happens ten years from now when I become too much trouble? Hell, it could happen in one year," she said. "I can't let you become my entire world. I won't go through that again."

Ignoring the fact that she didn't want him to touch her, Gage embraced her. "That won't happen. I'll never let you go."

She tilted her head back and her eyes met his. "You don't know that." She moved from his arms. "I'm going for a walk, alone," she told him as she started out of the room.

"Marissa." Gage stopped her with words even though he wanted to use force. "Don't—"

She sighed and interrupted him. "I won't leave the territory, but I wasn't asking for permission."

Gage watched her walk away. The woman who had stolen his heart and held it in her hands. He would love her forever. He could feel it and the wolf inside him agreed. He needed to be patient with her, that she had a lot to get past, but he needed her to start making her way to him. To his Pack. He needed her with him. It was more than just sexual. He needed her like he'd never needed another person.

And he wasn't certain he could suppress that need for long. As much he wanted to give her the space she needed, Gage wasn't built like that. Yes, he saw her as his equal and he was going to have to find a way to prove that to her. But she was also going to have to accept him as not only her mate but an Alpha as well.

He was born and trained for the job and he couldn't just switch it off.

There had to be a middle ground for them.

Marissa walked in the woods behind Gage's house. The farther she got, the more peaceful she felt. It was only yesterday that her life had changed. She had seen her old lover, taken a mate, and committed herself.

She had no intention of leaving. She knew her place was here with Gage. It was the Pack she still wasn't so certain about. No matter how hard she tried, she couldn't help but compare them to the one she'd grown up in. As happy as she wanted to be, there was something in her head telling her that it wouldn't last.

She'd hurt Gage with her words and that wasn't something she wanted to continue to do. Maybe she needed to talk about all her conflicting emotions. Gage would be the best one to speak to but she wanted someone who wasn't as invested as he was. Maybe Logan would have time to spend with her. He was Gage's best friend, so he could help her understand him better.

Happy to have made a decision that would hopefully bring them closer together, Marissa decided to enjoy what Gage's property had to offer before she went in search of her mate.

Marissa walked farther into the woods until she reached the creek that ran through the middle of the property. She sat at the edge and stared into the water. It rippled and flowed past her as she let her eyes close and felt herself drift.

It was beautiful here. Even though she couldn't shift and run like the others, she could still feel at peace. She could be happy here, with Gage, with her sister. She was so tired of being alone. For the first time in her life, she had more than just Elizabeth. She had a future, a chance, and an opportunity to have a family. This wasn't just Gage's territory but would be her home as well. She could take as many walks, come to the water, and roam whenever she wanted.

She'd also be able to spend more time with her sister. Maybe she and Elizabeth could become as close as they'd been as teenagers. When it was just them against the world.

Of course, they were both mated now so they no longer had to take on anyone without help. And wasn't that a nice thought?

A sound behind her had her opening her eyes and jumping to her feet. Marissa took in her surroundings, not seeing anything at first. When there was movement to her left, she turned and narrowed her eyes.

A man stepped out from between the trees and she tensed. He waved and Marissa recognized the guard from the first day. She'd seen him a couple of times since and he had always been friendly.

"Steve," she greeted after he'd walked to her.

"Sorry, didn't mean to startle you," he said as he smiled at her.

"No. No, it's okay. I guess I was lost in my own world."

"I could tell. You didn't even hear us approach."

"Us?" she asked, looking behind him.

"Us." His voice was joined by several growls. Three wolves stalked toward her while Steve opened his arms as if in a welcome. "Meet my friends."

Marissa backed as far as she could without falling into the creek. Steve and the wolves crept closer, and Marissa frantically tried to find a way out. The wolves snapped and growled at her.

"What's going on, Steve?" Marissa asked. She hadn't even prepared herself for an attack from one of Gage's Pack members. She'd been so busy worrying about Brandon that she'd let her guard down.

"It's nothing personal. I actually like you."

"Well, I don't think those wolves are the welcoming committee. Why are you doing this?" she demanded.

"Because I paid him."

Marissa was so surprised when Brandon stepped from the trees Steve had come from that she almost stumbled into the water.

Brandon laughed once she had righted herself. "Easy there, Marissa. Don't want you falling in now."

"Wh-what are you doing here?"

"Did you really think this was over? That you were done with me?" He took a step toward her. "I decide when we are finished."

"You already did. If I recall, you decided and then I was run out of the Pack," Marissa reminded him.

"Yes, well, I changed my mind. Who knew that you would turn out to be such a hottie? Or that you would fall in love with another Alpha?"

Realization hit Marissa. "That's what this is all about." She glared at Brandon. "You don't want me, you just don't want anyone else to have me."

Brandon appeared amused. His lips turned up and his eyes were shining. "Well, aren't you just a little conceited bitch?"

"Maybe, but I know I'm right." She looked from him to

the wolves. "So what's your plan here?"

"It's simple. You come with me quietly or I'll have the wolves tear you apart. After they are done with you, I will send them to your mate, and then your sister, and anyone else I think you care for."

"You wouldn't..." she said but didn't believe her own words. He was crazy. How had she never seen that before?

He smiled again and flashed his canines at her. "Oh, I would. I would."

"All right. I'll go with you." Marissa could only hope that someone would see her and stop Brandon from taking her. Maybe if she got close enough to Gage he'd be able to sense that something was wrong. She had to trust that her mate would be able to help her. If she tried to take out Brandon, the wolves would attack.

Marissa strode from the creek in the direction of the house, being careful not to get too close to Brandon. The wolves followed behind her.

Brandon let her pass between him and Steve. Marissa held her breath.

"Not that way." He grabbed her arm and yanked her to him.

"What?" She feigned ignorance.

"Not that way." Brandon started walking and pulled Marissa with him.

Forget playing along. She tried to dig her heels in, but her strength was no match for his. He easily dragged her as he marched in the opposite direction of the house. Away from Gage. No one would see them if they continued to head this way.

"Wait! What about my stuff?" Marissa tried to stall.

"Don't worry, you won't need anything," he assured her.

"What are you going to do with me?" Marissa had to fight even if it did mean an attack and possibly her death. She couldn't go back with him. There was no way she would survive. She had to trust Gage could protect himself, to watch over her sister. She just couldn't go with Brandon.

"Whatever I want," he said as he continued to take her farther away.

Desperate, Marissa did the only thing she could. She screamed as loud as possible. She didn't stop even as Brandon turned, pulled back his fist, then punched her. Her head snapped back and she tasted blood in her mouth.

"I told you to be quiet," he yelled, striking her again, knocking her off her feet.

Marissa wasn't going to be quiet. Screaming was the only way to let Gage know she was in trouble.

"Shut up!"

With a blow to the side of her head, Marissa's vision blurred. She put her hands in front of her, trying to ward off more blows.

Brandon stopped hitting her but pushed his weight on top of her. "I should have known better. You never did listen."

Marissa struggled but didn't have much fight left in her. "Get off me."

"I don't think so." He ran his hands over her body. "I should get to have a little fun with you before I feed you to the wolves."

Marissa didn't have the strength to stop him when his hand found its way under her shirt. Her stomach turned at the feel of his hands on her skin, but she wasn't dead yet and she would fight him with her last breath.

"I think you'll enjoy it too. Remember how good it was between us. How hot it was."

Marissa shook her head. "No. It wasn't that great. I've had better human lovers. And you don't even come close to Gage."

"You little bitch," Brandon spat, wrapping his hands around her neck.

As he squeezed, Marissa tried to grab his arms. Her nails scratched his bare forearms but he didn't release his hold on her.

"You need to get out of here." Steve's voice barely reached her from somewhere to her right. "Someone would have heard her scream. You have to leave before they come."

"It's too late for that." Gage's voice was the last thing Marissa heard before she passed out.

* * * *

Gage had been standing on his back porch with Logan, drinking a beer and staring into the woods when he'd heard Marissa's scream.

He didn't remember jumping off the porch or running to her. He didn't hear Logan behind him or Sam and the other guards change into wolf form. He just ran toward his mate.

All he could think about was Marissa being alone and afraid. Someone or something was attacking her. Possibilities ran through his mind as he used his supernatural speed to get to Marissa. Dread made him push himself harder and faster than before. Deep down, he just knew that Marissa had come across Brandon. He reached her and saw Brandon on top of her with his hands around her neck. She fought him like the true soldier she was. Taunting him with words when her strength wasn't enough. Hearing his guard Steve warn Brandon barely registered.

Brandon's head snapped up and their eyes met. Brandon looked at him defiantly, but Gage could also see the fear. It wasn't enough for him. He wanted the other man's hands off his mate.

"Let her go, *now!*" he ordered in a low, deadly voice.

Brandon glared down one last time before removing his hands from Marissa's neck. He stood and faced off with Gage.

"What are you going to do?" Brandon asked smugly, but his gaze flickered around. He knew he'd lost his one chance at taking Marissa and that Gage was going to make him pay.

Gage could see Logan standing by Steve, and his guards that were in wolf form had surrounded Brandon's wolves. The other Alpha was alone. It was just him and

Brandon now.

"Only what you deserve," Gage told him.

Brandon attacked. It was the opening Gage needed. Gage leapt toward him.

Both men changed in mid-air, coming down in wolf form, biting and fighting. Gage easily got the upper hand and had Brandon by the throat.

Brandon used his hind legs to claw at his stomach, but Gage held on tightly with his teeth. He could taste Brandon's blood gushing into his mouth and it was a heavenly victory. He shook his head, tearing the vulnerable throat even more.

A red haze clouded his mind as Brandon whimpered in his hold. Gage wanted to let all of his humanity go. To release himself fully to the wolf and allow the animal inside to have free rein. It was an instinct that he never fully gave in to. At that moment he couldn't come up with a reason to deny his wolf.

This was the one that had caused Marissa so much pain. The man who had put the fear and distrust into her eyes. He would rip out his throat for doing it to any female, but the fact that he'd done it to Gage's mate made him want to savor the moment.

That's when Gage felt the touch to his own neck and Marissa's sweet voice next to his ear. He froze as she crouched beside him.

"That's enough, Gage." She stroked his fur. "He's not worth it. Let him go and face the Council."

Gage growled, voicing his displeasure at her suggestion.

"Come on, baby. It will be more humiliating for him to have to face everyone than you killing him. He tried to take me against my will, he lost a fight with you, he will be finished as an Alpha. As well as being in any Pack."

Marissa continued to stroke his neck and legs. It was hard to keep his anger when his mate was so close to him. Gage wanted to turn into her embrace but he still had his enemy to deal with. Brandon had gone limp, the fight having gone out of him, but that wasn't enough for Gage. He wanted the other shifter to suffer.

"I need you...my mate," Marissa said. "Let Logan deal with Brandon."

Marissa needed him. That helped him make up his mind. Gage dropped the other wolf, whose head landed on the hard ground with a loud bang. He was unconscious but alive.

Gage nuzzled Marissa and she wrapped her arms around him. He had to make sure that she was uninjured. He sniffed her neck where that bastard had been choking her. He whimpered as he ran his tongue around her abused skin.

"It's okay," she whispered to him. "I'm okay."

Her words helped but Gage still needed to be certain. He pushed against her a little harder. Not enough to hurt but where she would know he wanted her to lie back.

"Okay," she agreed. She released him then laid on the cool grass.

Movement beside had him snapping his head over, but it was just Logan taking possession of Brandon. That was fine. Gage had other things to worry about. He crawled over to Marissa and laid his furry cheek along hers before he started his inspection.

He sniffed, licked, and rubbed her from head to toe before he was satisfied that his mate was unharmed. As soon as he sat back on his haunches, Marissa lifted up.

"Happy now?" she asked.

Gage shook his entire body before he stretched his front legs out and rested his chin on them. He stared up at Marissa, just taking in her beauty. Since he couldn't communicate with her in his shifted form, it was nice to be able to look at her.

"Oh, Gage." She laughed, then it was her crawling over to him.

Gage rolled onto his back and enjoyed her running her fingers through his fur and over his stomach. It wasn't a position he'd found himself in, ever. He wouldn't show submission to anyone other than his mate. But even in his wolf form he knew who Marissa was and wanted her touch.

He didn't know how long he lay there until Marissa finally patted his snout and stood.

"It's getting chilly and we need to deal with the fallout from Brandon's attack. You'd better shift back," she said.

Gage easily rose to his feet. He started his transformation. Just picturing himself as a human and he was changing. It was an easy process for him since he'd been shifting as long as he could remember.

He was a little shaky as he stood but Marissa was right there with her arms around him. Gage lowered his forehead to hers embracing her back.

"You're sure you're okay?" he asked her.

She tilted her head back and smiled. "Already healing. And you got here before he could really hurt me."

Gage was so fucking thankful for that. "I'm sorry he caught you alone. If I hadn't been acting like an ass it wouldn't have happened."

"I'm just as much to blame," she said. "I had no intention of leaving. I just let my anger get the better of me."

He smiled. "I guess we still have a few things to work on."

"Yes." She placed her hand in his and squeezed. "But I'm not going anywhere so we have plenty of time to figure things out."

Gage glanced around the empty clearing. Everyone else had left and it was only the two of them. He peered at Marissa with lust. He was already naked and it would be so easy to lose himself inside her body.

"Don't even think about it," she told him. "We have got to get back to the house and be responsible."

He grumbled even though he knew she was right.

"Come on." She tugged on his hand so they could start the walk back to the house.

Chapter Nine

Marissa ran between the trees, zigzagging and crossing her scent so it would be hard to tell which way she ran. The wolf chasing her was so close she could practically feel his warm breath on her. She jumped over a fallen log and changed directions, heading to the creek.

She hadn't wanted to go back to that place after the events from the day before but Gage had insisted that they returned. He didn't want any area on the property that she was afraid or uncomfortable in. So, after breakfast in their room, they'd decided to play a game to try to wipe away Brandon's attack.

When the water came into view, she used the last of her energy and raced toward it. If she could beat Gage there in her human form that would give her some bragging rights — even if he had given her a ten minute start.

Before reaching it, she was knocked to the ground when the wolf's large bulk hit her. Marissa rolled as she fell and ended up on her back. Her breath came out in pants from the long, hard run.

The wolf stood over her, licking her face.

"Stop, Gage. Stop!" She pushed him away, laughing.

He gave a fake growl and settled down next to her. It was a comfort to have him right beside her. She was glad she'd agreed to come out this morning. The cool morning breeze blew across her heated body while she closed her eyes and breathed in the sweet air.

Marissa hoped they would have more times like this. She knew that Gage was extremely busy but had been putting all of his business on hold for her. She couldn't let that continue. He needed to take care of his Pack while she settled in.

After Gage's father had been called to collect Brandon, Steve and the other wolves, Marissa had retired to her new bedroom and let Gage handle the details. It was still hard for her to think about Brandon's attack.

Would he really have killed her? She wanted to believe that he wouldn't have but Marissa wasn't so sure. Even as he'd been dragged away Brandon had been claiming her as his own.

It was creepy and terrifying but Gage had slipped his arm around her waist and held her tight.

Now the Council was sending representatives and Brandon's dad had been called. In addition to Gage needing to get back to his Pack, they also had to prepare for the trials that would be coming up.

Luckily shifter justice worked a whole lot faster than the American system. By the end of the week a decision would be made about Brandon and the others. Gage was still upset that one of his own guards had sold them out. Logan had questioned the guard and found out that for a thousand dollars he'd let Brandon inside the property.

Marissa was glad that it hadn't been Gage who'd gotten that information. By the amount of cursing and items broken in Gage's office, it was easy to see that the Alpha hadn't taken that news well at all.

Gage licked her arm and she opened her eyes to peer over at him.

"You are so beautiful like this," she said. The day before she had been so worried that he was going to kill Brandon that she'd forgotten to tell him.

It was unusual for her to be able to appreciate anyone in their shifted form. She was normally so filled with jealousy that she couldn't even stand to be around anyone shifted, not even her own sister. But Gage had changed that for her. She could now begin to accept her shortcomings and try to make a better future for her and Gage.

She hadn't even told him thank you. "Change back," she ordered, ready for some of the human fun they had come out here for. Her body already tingled with need for her mate.

Gage dipped his head before he began his transformation. It was a sight to watch. How his body contorted and his human skin replaced the fur. It was quick and painless when Gage did it. She always wondered, though, how it would be for her.

Once in human form, he collapsed on top of her, his erection digging into her hip. She giggled and rubbed along him. This should be fun.

"Is my little wolf hungry?" he asked, raising his body just a fraction from her.

Marissa grasped the base of his cock and stroked him. "Always. Always hungry for you," she admitted. It was nice to have someone who wanted her just as much as she craved him. She tightened her hold as she pumped him faster.

He thrust against her hand then pulled away from her.

Marissa pouted at him. "I was just starting to have fun."

"It's my turn, though," he said before he slammed his mouth over hers and pushed his tongue inside. He covered his body with hers once again but this time he used his knees to push her thighs apart.

Marissa sucked on his tongue, drawing out a moan from him. She moved her hands down his back until she could grip his ass tightly. He bucked against her then lifted his head.

"I'm already naked," he said. "But you seem to be wearing way too many clothes."

She laughed and wiggled while she helped him remove all of her garments.

Once she was naked with him kneeling between her legs, she reached up and cupped his face. "Remember the last time we did this outside?"

"Oh yeah." He gripped the base of his cock and stroked.

"Every detail."

"Are we going to be interrupted again?" she asked as she placed her palm over his.

Gage laughed. "I'm pretty sure Logan knows that I'll hurt him if he pulls a stunt like that. Or allows anyone else close."

"Good," Marissa said when she lay back. This time she didn't need help to open her legs. She spread her thighs wide, allowing him to see every intimate part of her. She raised her hands to her breasts and began to knead. "Take me, mate me."

With hands shaking, he pushed her knees up to her chest and positioned himself at her entrance. Gage leaned forward to run his tongue over her bottom lip then plunged it inside, swallowing her cry.

His cock slid in and out of her and Marissa tightened her inner muscles to try to keep him inside. Gage went wild. He was panting and grunting as he plunged inside over and over.

Marissa dug her heels into the soil while lifting her hips to rock into each thrust. She moved her hands from her body to press against his chest. His heart was pounding and sweat was beginning to slick his body.

With another rough slam of his body, Marissa closed her eyes and arched. Perfect, oh that was it. "Gage!" she cried out and climaxed.

"Not done," he said before he rocked his hips even faster.

"Uh!" she screamed when he rode her through her orgasm and continued to plunge deep. Her clit was tingling and her breasts were full. If Gage kept up this pace she was going to come again.

"More? Can you take it?" he asked while slowing down.

"Don't stop!" she demanded. "Don't you dare!"

"God, I love you," he told her then reared and started to slam back, regaining his frantic pace.

Her entire body was being rocked by his movements and she had to lower her hands to the ground to try to find a way to hold on.

"Almost there," he cried.

Marissa bit her bottom lip, raised her hips and allowed him to really pound her.

Gage's head fell forward as he growled, then he was coming. The warmth from his seed was just enough to send her over the edge into a second orgasm. He shook until he was done filling her with his essence.

"I love you too," she managed to get out.

Gage laughed. "What a pair the two of us make."

"Yeah," she agreed. "We're perfect together."

The silence around them was peaceful, and Marissa wondered how long they could stay like that. Wouldn't it be nice to just hide from the world wrapped up in her mate's arms?

"We've been gone a long time," Gage said. "We should probably think about getting in."

Well, there went that fantasy. Marissa nodded although she made no move to get up. Gage chuckled, nuzzling her neck.

"I don't want to either but I have to check in with Logan. Hopefully the Council will arrive soon and then we can put this behind us," he said.

"Then what?" she asked, still unsure about her future in the Pack.

"I would like to collect your things from California and get you moved in here officially," Gage answered quietly.

She turned her head. He was sitting up peering down at her.

"I know it's a big change for you. I'll be with you the entire time but I want to start our life together," Gage said.

So did she. "I know. I do need some more clothes," she teased.

"Well, let's not go crazy," he laughed. "I like you this way."

"Speaking of being naked, are you going to walk back to the house like that?" she asked.

Gage grinned then winked. "Come on."

It was a good thing that the Pack stashed clothes all over the property for when they shifted. Gage would have hated to ask Marissa to carry something for him to change into. Not that he minded walking around without clothes, but with the amount of Pack that were coming and going while cleaning up from the party the previous night, he really didn't want to just stroll up to his house completely bared.

Plus, his dad was probably back and that just wasn't a moment he wanted with his father. While still hidden by the trees, he stopped and grabbed a backpack full of clothes. As he dressed he kept his eyes on Marissa.

She seemed to be dealing with the attack yesterday pretty well and that worried him. Shouldn't she be freaking out or refusing to go to the creek? Instead, it had barely taken him anything to get her to agree. He wanted to replace the memories of Brandon with good ones but now Gage was uncertain if he'd been right.

After pulling on a pair of sweats and a T-shirt, Gage tugged Marissa close. "You doing okay?" he asked.

"Yeah," she agreed quickly. Maybe too quickly?

Gage wasn't buying it. He stepped in front of her when she went to walk by him. Marissa paused before she glanced up at him.

"Talk to me," he pleaded.

She blew out a long breath. "I don't know what to say," she said.

Gage nodded to encourage her to talk.

"I thought he was going to take me, and I thought I was going to die."

"Oh, baby." He reached for her.

"No." She shook her head. "Wait."

Gage dropped his hand back down to his side.

Marissa turned and paced away then back. "I cared."

He didn't get it. "Cared?" he asked.

"I didn't want to die!" she exclaimed.

Well, he hoped not. "Okay?"

"You don't understand," she accused.

He really couldn't argue that point. "Then explain it to me."

She huffed. "I didn't want to die but before I met you I..." She shrugged.

Ah, he got it now. Gage wouldn't let her push him away this time. He grabbed her shoulder and yanked her to him. As he dipped his head she appeared confused. He didn't mind that at all. He kissed her deeply, hoping to show her just how important she was to him.

Once Marissa was thrusting her tongue against his and moving slower, Gage drew back. Her cheeks were flushed and even if they'd just made love he knew he could have her again. That wasn't the point he was trying to make, though.

"Before you met me you were alone and thought no one would miss you," he said for her.

"I had Elizabeth but—"

"But she has her own life. She would have been heartbroken but still you knew she'd eventually get over the loss of you," he finished.

"Yeah," Marissa told him.

"Now you know that I couldn't live without you," Gage spoke sternly. "I need you in my life like no one else ever has."

"I still think you're making a mistake with me," Marissa said.

Gage snorted. "You're a smart woman but sometimes you say the stupidest things."

Marissa narrowed her eyes.

"You're it for me," Gage said. "If Brandon had taken you, hurt you more than he did, I would have destroyed him and his entire Pack."

He liked it when she shivered. It was time that he showed her the Alpha side of him. So far that had been limited to bed but Marissa was now mated to an Alpha. She was part of the inner circle.

"I don't know how to respond when you say things like that," she admitted.

"You don't have to say a thing," he assured her. "But I'm an Alpha and you're my mate. This is our life. You are more important to me than anything else. The days of you being alone and only having to worry about yourself are over."

Marissa stared at him for several seconds then finally nodded. Gage smiled. It felt like they'd made progress in their relationship.

"Now, let's get back to the house," he said as he took her hand in his. "If we're gone too long Logan will probably send out a search party."

"You just said that he wouldn't let anyone near us," she pointed out. "You know, when we were..." She waved her hand around.

Gage smirked. "I did say that, didn't I?"

She swatted his arm with her free hand and giggled. "You're so bad."

He loved the sound of her being happy. It was his job to make sure that she was always safe and happy. Gage took his responsibilities seriously so he knew he wouldn't fail her again.

As they strolled out of the woods, Gage could see that Logan, his father and another man were sitting out on the back porch. He grinned. It looked like Marissa was going to get to meet his friend Cain sooner than he'd thought.

"Who's that?" she asked. Her eyes were narrowed like she was straining to see.

"How far does your sight go?" he questioned. He really needed to learn more about the non-shifter part of her.

She glanced over at him. "What?"

"Your eyesight," he repeated. "How good is it?"

"Oh," she said. "Better than a full human's but not as good as yours."

"Sense of smell?" he asked.

"What is this, twenty questions?" she asked, frowning.

He squeezed her hand. "I want to know everything about you," he told her.

"That's...um..." She was beautiful when she was caught off guard. "Okay."

"So?" he pressed when she didn't answer his question.

"Scent is my strongest feature," she said. "It's still not as good as a full shifter but nowhere near as bad as a human."

"You are a full shifter," he said. That kind of thinking was the first that needed to go.

"One that can't shift," she said with bitterness.

"You can't transform into your wolf but you told me before that you still feel the animal," he said.

"Yes," she said.

"So you are a shifter," he told her. "You need to get used to thinking that way."

Marissa didn't respond but he'd give her time. They'd almost reached the men on the porch. Cain was the first to stand then Logan and his father.

"Hey, man," Gage greeted his old friend. "I'm grateful you could make it." He had to release Marissa's hand as Cain lifted him in a bone-crushing hug.

"Of course," Cain replied. He dropped Gage back down before he turned to Marissa.

Cain dipped his head in a sign of respect. "You must be Marissa. Gage is already talking about nothing but you."

Marissa appeared shocked by Cain's respectful greeting but she recovered well. "I would like to thank you for coming as well. It's nice to meet you." She held out her hand and they shook.

Gage looked on, delighted. She had handled the meeting perfectly as an Alpha mate.

"To threaten an Alpha's mate is unacceptable," Cain stated firmly. "I am more than happy to be here. No one else will come after you."

"Perfectly said," Gage's father commented. "We were just sharing some coffee as we discussed the recent events. Join us?"

It hadn't really been a request so Gage placed his hand on Marissa's lower back and led her over to the wicker furniture. He chose the small bench that would allow them to sit together.

Marissa sat first and even though he'd settled next to her she still shifted closer. Gage held in his smile but did wrap his arm around her shoulder. Just then Hannah came out through the sliding glass door carrying two mugs.

He went to stand to take them from her but she tsked him.

"You sit there next to your mate and let me serve you," Hannah demanded.

"Yes, ma'am," he said with a dip of his head. He might be an Alpha but he made sure that he always showed respect to his elders. There weren't many wolf shifters that were as powerful as he. His father, of course, and Cain's, but very few could challenge Gage. Still, he expected his entire Pack to protect and care for their aging members.

Hannah smiled then set the mugs on the small table beside Gage. "Now, I have some homemade muffins in the oven so you drink these while I tend to them."

"Oh, you don't have to go to so much trouble," Marissa said. "We ate breakfast earlier."

"Don't you worry about it," Hannah said kindly. "It makes me feel good to be able to cook for you all. Just eat what you're hungry for." She winked. "I'm sure these boys can finish the rest."

Gage and Cain chuckled.

"Well, thank you," Marissa said. "I haven't had anything homemade in what seems like forever."

"It's about time we changed that," Hannah said with a pat to Marissa's arm.

As Hannah left them, Gage passed Marissa her cup of coffee. Marissa breathed in the scent before taking a small sip. He watched her, enjoying the sight. He didn't think he'd ever tire of seeing her do such mundane things.

Cain cleared his throat, drawing Gage's attention. He refused to be embarrassed getting caught admiring his mate.

"Any news?" Gage asked.

"Brandon's father arrived along with a couple of lawyers in tow," Gage's father said. "I believe that they met with Brandon this morning."

"He's still in jail, though?" Gage questioned.

His dad nodded. "We're lucky that the sheriff is mated to a shifter and is allowing us to use the cells there. We might need to think about having some place here that we can use in the future, though. Sheriff Thomas is thinking about retiring."

Gage nodded in agreement. He was lucky that his Pack was located away from any large cities. He was inside the Ector county territory but the number of residents was under ten thousand. Plus, most of the human residents were either mated or related to a shifter by marriage. The few that did not have any connection to the Pack didn't have a clue about them.

The small number of residents had a lot of property. This was oil field territory and the ranches were spread far and wide. If Gage didn't keep tabs on those that lived around his property he might never meet them.

But he was a careful Alpha and not only did he know all his neighbors but the residents of the three closest cities as well.

His father was right, though. Sheriff Thomas was in his sixties with a dozen grandchildren that would love to spend more time with him. If another friend of the Pack wasn't elected to take over when the Sheriff left they might have issues.

Gage liked using the small jail because it was on the other side of the county from his property. There was no way that he would allow Brandon anywhere near Marissa. So building a holding area inside the property would need more thought.

"We need to prepare for the Council representatives coming to town," his father said.

"We can accommodate them," Gage assured him. "There are plenty of homes."

"No." His father shook his head. "They won't stay near you or Brandon's Pack. I think it will be best if they stay in town. That way no one can accuse us of tampering with the judges."

"They'd be stupid to accuse the Council of wrongdoing," Cain stated.

Gage agreed.

"I think they've already proven that they are," his father responded.

"I'll call the Twin Bear bed and breakfast. There are only five rooms so it's small and run by humans," Logan said.

"Twin bears?" Cain asked.

Logan smiled. "The owners are brothers that believe their spirit animals are bears. They're good guys and completely harmless. Just eccentric."

"Sounds like my kind of place," Cain said, laughing.

"How many Council members are coming?" Gage asked.

"Three plus their guards. If we can get all of the rooms that should be plenty," his father answered.

"It's the slow season so I don't see a problem but I'll call right away," Logan said, standing. He pulled his phone from his pocket and stepped a few feet away.

Gage met Cain's gaze. "This is going to be a fucking mess."

Cain nodded. "This is an extremely important charge. We've always taken for granted that an Alpha wouldn't go into another's Pack and commit a crime like this. Even challenges from Packs and territories have to be approved by the Council. A lot of Alphas are going to pay close attention to what happens here. My father being one."

"There's a reason that we've been able to remain hidden for so long," his father added. "What Brandon did put all of us and our laws in danger. I don't see his punishment not being severe."

Gage glanced over at Marissa to check how she was

handling the conversation. She had a tight grip on her mug but her hands were still shaking. She looked up at him.

"This is all my fault," she said.

Gage growled but it was Cain who spoke up. "That's bullshit. From what I've heard your birth Pack has done everything wrong with you from the beginning."

Marissa gasped.

"No one, shifter, non-shifter, or human would have ever been treated the way you were," Cain said. "You should have been protected and embraced by the Pack."

She darted her gaze in Gage's direction before she looked back at Cain. "Have you ever met another non-shifter?" she asked quietly.

"Yes," Cain told her. "Not in my Pack but we're close to another who has two non-shifters. An elderly man and a pre-teen female. They are treated just like everyone else."

Marissa shook her head while cuddling closer to Gage. "I thought you were the only one who would accept me," she said to him. "I figured you and your Pack were unique."

"I know," Gage said. He was glad that she could see that what had happened to her was wrong. It was about time she accepted that the Pack she had been raised in was plain and simply evil.

"I have also met a couple of non-shifters," his dad said. "They haven't had easy lives but none have been mistreated like you. Would you like to meet them someday?"

She bit her lip as she considered the offer. "I think so."

Hannah opened the door carrying out a plate of fresh and hot muffins. Since Gage had shifted earlier he'd burned off his breakfast and was starving. Hannah set the platter down along with some smaller plates.

"Now I expect you all to eat these up," she said. "I have some more in the oven. We'll have a lot of visitors so you need to keep your energy up."

They all nodded and she smiled before she returned to the kitchen.

"God, I love coming here," Cain said as he leaned forward

and picked up one of the hot blueberry muffins. "Hannah is such an awesome cook."

"It's one of the things I miss," his dad agreed.

Gage exchanged an amused look with Marissa while placing one of the muffins on a plate before passing it to her. Then he filled his own plate with two. As he bit into the moist food he moaned. The blueberry flavor burst on his tongue and was wonderful.

Cain and his father were also chowing down while Marissa remained picking at hers.

Gage nudged her arm. "You'd better at least eat one or you'll hurt Hannah's feelings."

Marissa nodded then took a bite.

Good. Gage thought that Marissa could gain a few more pounds. She was beautiful but he also wanted her healthy.

Not having someone take care of her had resulted in her being on the thin side. Even though he knew he couldn't right all the wrongs in her life he wanted to try.

After she'd taken the first bite, eating seemed to come easier to her. She even asked for a second.

Pleased, Gage enjoyed his own snack.

Chapter Ten

Hannah had been correct when she'd said that they'd have a lot of visitors. Marissa couldn't even count how many hands she'd shaken or hugs given to her. It had seemed like a long day with everyone wishing her the best and telling her she had their support.

Now that it was late into the night she finally had a minute to herself. Gage had taken her to bed earlier and showed her how much he loved and craved her. Marissa had always had a pretty active love life but Gage was insatiable. She'd never had a lover like him. He was rough yet gentle at the same time. She had no idea how that was possible but he managed it. She'd never felt more cared for than she had the last several days.

Which was what was keeping her from sleeping.

She'd slipped from bed and showered before dressing in soft sleep bottoms and a loose T-shirt. She was bare-footed and her hair was still wet but since it was past midnight she didn't expect to run into anyone.

Gage had been telling her for days that this was her home now and she needed to be comfortable. So she was heading to the kitchen to see what she could snack on. Marissa wasn't actually hungry but she needed to think, and being wrapped up in Gage's arms was too distracting at the moment.

The more she relaxed inside the Alpha house and with Gage, the more Marissa was starting to wonder if she was losing her edge. She'd always taken care of herself and to have to rely on someone else was strange. Plus, she didn't have just herself to worry about. Now she had a mate that she was putting in danger.

If Gage was hurt by this it would be all her fault. How could she live with herself?

Marissa pushed open the swinging kitchen door but paused on the threshold. Gage's dad sat at the large island with a plate of cookies and a tall glass of milk.

"I'm sorry," she said quietly. "I didn't think anyone else was up."

He waved her forward. "Come keep me company as I break my diet. I swear by the time I leave I'm going to have gained twenty pounds."

She grinned as she strolled forward. Being a shifter, Gage's dad would burn off the calories that he consumed. Marissa, on the other hand, had to watch what she ate. Not being able to shift affected every part of her life. She had no idea how she was going to make it inside the Pack.

"Sit," Gage's father told her. "I'll get you a glass of milk. That's the best way to enjoy some of Hannah's chocolate chip cookies."

"Oh no," she said. "You don't have to do that."

He lifted a brow. The same way that his son did. "Are you going to make me eat these alone?"

He sounded amused but she still felt like it was a challenge. "Okay," she agreed before she climbed up on the stool next to him.

"Good girl," he praised.

Warmth spread through her at his approval. It was foreign to feel this way.

He went to the cabinet to pull down a glass and she watched him. He was probably in his sixties but he moved around like a young man. There was a small spring to his step as he moved around.

After he'd filled her glass he set it in front of her then sat back down. He pushed the plate closer to her. Marissa picked up one of the cookies and studied it, trying to think of something to say. She barely knew the man and was sleeping with his son. What should they talk about?

"You don't have to say anything," he told her as if reading her mind. "We can sit here and enjoy these freshly baked cookies then go up to our own rooms and not have to talk."

That sounded good. "Or?"

"Or," he said, "you can tell me what's on your mind. What is keeping you awake while you should be asleep next to your mate?"

"Are you mad that he mated a non-shifter?" The question was out of her mouth before she'd realized what she was going to ask.

Gage's father shook his head. "On the contrary, I couldn't imagine a better mate for him."

She snorted. "Yeah right."

He grinned before he picked up a cookie for himself. "You don't have to believe me but I think you will soon enough."

When he didn't elaborate Marissa fidgeted. She had to know what he meant. "Why?" she finally asked.

"My son has been a member of this Pack his entire life," he said. "He's a strong leader but he's never come across a real challenge. Most shifters wouldn't even consider challenging such a strong wolf shifter but times are changing."

"What do you mean?" she questioned.

"The world that we've been living in," he answered. "There's been a lot of grumbling between the different shifter factions. They're tired of hiding, sick of being hunted down when in their animal form. Something is going to have to change. I don't know if it'll be in a year, five, or twenty but eventually all Alphas are going to have to help protect shifters. Gage will need a strong partner by his side when the time comes."

"He'll be fine," she said. "He has more compassion than anyone I've ever met."

"I agree with you. And Gage won't back down if it comes to protecting anyone. But at what cost? How long will he remain fair and compassionate with so much responsibility? If there is no one to take care of him then how can he stay strong?" he asked.

"Gage doesn't need anyone to take care of him," she said.

"That's where you're wrong. But I have no doubt that you'll learn. An Alpha needs a partner more than anyone else in the Pack. He's had and will have more tough decisions to make. He needs someone he can trust who will always be on his side."

"Logan… Cain…" she said.

"Rely on him to make the decisions. Only you will try to protect him at all costs," he responded.

"There have to be dozens of females who'd be better at it than me," she confessed. "I've never been in a Pack like this."

"Ah." He grinned as he pointed at her. "That's right. And that's why you're perfect."

"I don't understand," she admitted.

"How many women could have withstood what you did? First the abuse in the Pack—and what you went through was abuse. Then on your own for ten years. I know strong male shifters that wouldn't have been able to handle that. You're going to make Gage stronger because you are a survivor."

Was that true? Marissa didn't know what to say so she didn't say anything at all. Instead, she thought about what Gage's father had said.

Marissa did believe herself strong. Of course, she'd also considered herself broken and defective. If she was to trust what Gage's dad said then she would have to rethink everything she'd once thought was fact.

One thing that she could say for certain was that Gage's dad was correct in saying that she would protect Gage. If he had to be strong for everyone else then she would be there for him when he had finished his duties. That was what she could do for her mate.

"I can see that you're thinking about it already," Gage's father said. "That's good."

She glanced at him.

"You're going to be tested during this trial. You will get

through it. Let my son help you," he said.

Marissa nodded.

"I mean it. This isn't just about Brandon's attack. The entire Pack, especially the inner circle, is going to have to explain their behavior toward you and your sister."

"Elizabeth's on her honeymoon," Marissa said. "She doesn't need to be involved in this."

"I'm sorry but there's a good chance that the Council is going to want to talk to her."

"Damn," she muttered. It appeared that she'd screwed up Elizabeth's life once again.

"Logan already called Greg and they're on the way back. Your sister was more worried about you than she cared about her trip."

"Still," she said. "This is supposed to be a special time for her."

"It will be," he assured her. "Logan already spoke to Greg and offered him the use of the family cabin up in the mountains in California. I think it'll be nice for them."

Oh wow, that was cool.

"Plus, after all of this is over, you and your sister will be safe and together. I believe that's more important to her than a few days away."

Yeah, that sounded good to Marissa too.

"Did this talk help?" he asked.

"Yes," she admitted. "Can I ask you one more question?"

"You can ask me as many as you want," he told her. "We're family now."

Marissa had to smile at that. "Family," she repeated. Other than Elizabeth, she didn't have anyone else who'd ever cared what happened to her. Now it appeared that Gage wasn't the only one that she was adding to her life.

"Yes, now ask your question," he said.

"How does a trial work? I don't know what to expect," she said.

"Good," he replied. "That's a smart question. What will happen is the Council members will act as the judges. We'll go over the charges and the Council will talk to everyone involved."

"Will you be there?" she questioned.

"No, since you're family I can't be on the judging committee. Plus, I'm a witness also. I came down here before the attack on you because there was a threat to my son and his mate. Brandon's father called me and we spoke about Brandon leaving. I'll tell them everything I saw and heard."

"What do I say?" she asked.

"Tell them exactly what happened that day by the creek. Then when asked about how you were treated growing up, just be honest."

"I can do that," she murmured. "Especially if it will keep Brandon away from Gage."

"I have no doubt that Brandon will be found guilty. I just want to make sure that his father and the Pack also pay for how they treated you and your sister."

"It's that important to you?" she asked. Why so many people cared about the way she'd been raised confused her.

"Yes." He nodded. "Not only because it is to Gage but because when an Alpha fails to protect a Pack member he breaks his word. Our entire society is based on having an Alpha do his job. It also worries me that even more is going on there and maybe other shifters are being hurt or not taken care of."

"I never thought about that," she said. "I stayed away from most everyone except Brandon."

"From what you've said I'm surprised that you hooked up with him."

"I know," she agreed. "I spent a lot of time on my own. Brandon would come around and talk to me. Eventually we spent all of our free time together."

"If his attention had been for the good I would praise him. Now I think he was just using you."

"Yeah," she said. "But maybe he did me a favor."

"How's that?" he asked.

"If I hadn't gone through what I did maybe Elizabeth would have never left the Pack. She wouldn't have started dating Greg and I wouldn't have met Gage," she explained.

He hugged her. She was so surprised she just froze. He laughed, but not unkindly.

"You're going to be fine. Now you better get some rest. I expect the Council members here tomorrow and they'll want to start the trial right away."

Marissa glanced down and realized that not only had she finished her milk but she had also eaten several cookies. She stood and grabbed her glass.

"I'll clean up," Gage's father told her. "You just get some sleep."

She nodded then clearly surprised him by hugging him hard. He patted her back and Marissa could have wept with joy. This must be what it would have been like to have a dad.

"Go now," he said then pushed her toward the door.

Marissa followed his order and made her way back to Gage.

* * * *

Gage had gotten out of bed earlier when he'd woken without Marissa. He'd panicked and had almost fallen out of the bed. As soon as he'd gotten control of himself he'd raced to the door and used his heightened senses to locate her.

She'd been in the kitchen with his father. He hadn't been able to make out the words but the murmur of their talking had calmed him. He'd fought the urge to go to her and had crawled back into bed to wait. Now that he was lying there awake he finally had time to think about the day.

He was proud of his Pack and the support they'd shown him and his new mate. It was obvious that Marissa had been overwhelmed at times but she'd dealt with the excess of people like a champ. He hadn't doubted she'd make a good

Alpha mate and the day had proven that he was correct. Right away he'd noticed that she was most comfortable with the teenagers who had approached her. He knew Elizabeth loved children as she worked at the elementary school. Marissa seemed to hit it off with the teenagers. Gage was certain that would come in handy in the future. Most of the Pack teenagers avoided him as he was the ultimate parental figure but if they could go to his mate Gage felt secure that they'd be able to help more of the Pack.

Smiling, he reclined against the headboard and picked up his e-reader from the nightstand. He'd been looking forward to the latest novel from his favorite suspense author and as he waited for his mate he'd be able to get started.

Two chapters down and he was fully engaged in the mystery and intrigue of the spy world when the bedroom door opened.

"What are you doing?" she asked as she closed the door behind her.

Gage powered off his device. "I woke up and you weren't here. It scared me."

"Oh! I'm sorry," she said while rushing to him. "I didn't even think about that. I just couldn't sleep."

When she got close enough, Gage reached out and grabbed her wrist. He tugged her down onto his lap. "It's not your fault. If you want to wander around the house in the middle of the night you have every right. Even sneak off to eat Hannah's cookies."

She smiled. "How'd you know that?"

"I went to find you but picked up on you and my father in the kitchen. If Dad's up this late then he's been in the cookie jar," Gage told her. "That's his weakness. I think Hannah makes fresh cookies just to tempt him."

Marissa nodded. "Yeah, he was enjoying them."

Gage leaned forward and sniffed. "He wasn't the only one."

"Well," she said. "I might have had a couple."

"Good," Gage said. He settled back to get more

comfortable. "Did you have a good talk with my dad?"

"Why didn't you come down?" she asked.

"I figured if you got the chance to talk to my father it might help with whatever was keeping you up," Gage answered. "He gives really good advice over milk and cookies."

"He does," she said. "And yes, we had a good talk. I'm glad he was there. You're very lucky."

"You don't talk about your parents," Gage said. Now that he thought about it, neither did Elizabeth. The only time he could recall Elizabeth mentioning her parents was when they'd first met and she'd wanted to join the Pack. He'd asked about her family and she'd told him that her parents weren't around, then gone on to explain that her sister was rogue.

"There's not much to say," Marissa told him. "My dad left us and the Pack when it became obvious that something was wrong and I couldn't shift. My mom blamed me. After that she wasn't around a lot. When she was it wasn't good. She stayed drunk or high. Elizabeth and I raised ourselves."

"Do you know where they are now?" he asked.

"No," Marissa said. "I never saw my dad again and my mom just left one night and never came back. Elizabeth went to the Alpha but there was nothing we could do. She was an adult and had already been taking care of me. My mom didn't contribute anything to the Pack anyway. She didn't pay the fees and Elizabeth worked two jobs so she could pay him so we'd be able to stay."

Gage didn't realize he was growling until she rubbed his chest and soothed him.

"It's okay," she whispered. "We made it through."

"The more I hear, the bigger the urge to rip the throat out of your old Alpha."

She surprised him by laughing. "I won't say that I never had that thought because, honestly, the man's a prick. But he'll face the Council and they'll decide if he should suffer a punishment."

"You really were talking to my dad," Gage said.

Marissa seemed just a bit different. More confident and steadier than she'd been.

"He's a smart guy," she said. "I can see why you make such a good Alpha with a teacher like him."

It made him pleased and proud for Marissa to say that. His father was the best person he knew and Gage could only pray that he'd be as good an Alpha as him.

"Is there anything you want to talk about?" Gage asked her. With the way Marissa was opening up, he wanted to unlock the lines of communication.

"Can I ask you a question?"

"Of course," he replied quickly.

"What kind of mate do you expect me to be?" she asked.

Gage didn't really need to think hard about his answer. "I want an equal partner," he said. "Someone who accepts my dominant side but is also able to stand by their convictions and give me their opinion."

She laughed.

"You've been doing it from the moment we met," he said.

"You mean I'm a pain in the ass," she teased.

"Yes," he agreed with a wink. "That's how I knew I'd never be bored. You're strong and independent but you also care about those around you. I watched you with our Pack today. You welcomed them into your life. I don't know if you even realize it."

"I didn't at the time but when I thought about it I felt like I'd made the first step to joining the Pack," she said.

"You're already Pack," Gage told her.

"To you and maybe to your Pack," she said. "But I still didn't feel it until I saw you surrounded by the Pack and looking over at me like I was your world. That's when I knew."

"And made you question your place," he guessed. "Which is why you were awake."

"I don't want you or the Pack to suffer because of me," she said.

"We need you more than what we would suffer," he said.

"I need you."

"I know," she told him. "Your dad helped me realize that I could help you."

"Really?" he asked. He'd have to thank his father in the morning for whatever he'd said.

"You need someone to be on your side," she said. "Who will protect you above all else."

Gage beamed at her. "I do."

"So that's my job," she said.

"What else do you want to do?" he asked. She'd given him the perfect opportunity to bring up a subject he'd wanted to broach.

"Do?" she asked.

"What are you interested in?" he clarified. "I know you work in an office now. Do you want to work with me here or out of the house? We have several businesses that you could work at."

"I don't know," she said slowly. "I need to think about it. I haven't really had the opportunity to explore. I worked fast food, restaurants, and then started to take temp jobs in offices before I got my current position."

"You'll have plenty of time to decide," he promised. "I just wanted you to know that you can do whatever it is that you want. I'll support you. I want you to be happy."

"I will be," she said. Marissa leaned forward to brush her lips over his.

Gage ran his hand down her shoulder before he threaded his fingers through her hair. He held her still as he plundered her mouth with his tongue. Marissa was moaning and clawing at his chest. He hadn't dressed so her nails dug into his flesh with a bite of pain. He lifted his hips to drag his erection against her.

"I have to have you," he said.

"Then take me," she replied breathlessly.

Gage rolled her onto her back then lifted enough to rip the sheets between them away.

"Arms up," he ordered.

She complied and he pushed her T-shirt up and over her head. Gage leaned down and captured one of her pert nipples in his mouth. She arched into him while he sucked. He forgot all about the top once her beautifully smooth skin was revealed. He continued to kiss from one breast to the other, running his hands down to push off the cotton bottoms she'd put on.

Marissa raised her hips, helping him by shimmying out of them. Gage sat back to peer at her.

She was flushed and breathing hard. The T-shirt had twisted around her wrists, giving him a devious idea. Gage reached up and tangled the material tighter before he pressed her wrists against the mattress.

"What are you doing?" she asked.

Gage grinned. "Keep them there," he ordered.

She was already nodding before he'd even finished his sentence.

"Good girl," he praised.

Now that he had her at his mercy, Gage slid down her body and spread her thighs, opening her up for his view. She was already wet so he slipped one finger through her folds to spear into her pussy.

"Oh," she gasped.

He wanted a better reaction than that. Gage lowered himself between her legs so that he could reach her with his tongue. He held her thighs wide, swiping at her opening. She hissed before she grabbed the back of his head and forced him down on her harder.

Gage licked up her juices, enjoying her flavor as it burst over his tongue. She tasted sweet. Her legs shook but Gage didn't stop. He knew how to bring his mate pleasure. As he added a finger, Gage wrapped his arm around one of her thighs to keep her still. Marissa was trying to buck up but he wanted her to have to take what he gave her. Marissa's arms were still over her head so he was happy she was following his directions.

He brought her to the edge of climax then backed off,

removing his mouth and fingers.

"No!" she cried out, reaching for him.

Gage caught her wrists and pushed them back to the mattress. "Keep them there."

"Please," she begged beautifully.

Gage lowered his head so he could brush his lips over hers. When she opened for him he once again lifted away.

"Ugh," she protested.

He just grinned down at her. She stuck her lower lip out in a pout and he laughed. It wasn't an expression that he thought he'd see on her face.

"What?" he teased while trailing a finger down her stomach.

"I want you," she said.

"I know," he replied. He was throbbing with need but he also enjoyed this little game.

"So stop teasing me!" she demanded.

Gage lifted a brow. "Who's the Alpha?"

Marissa huffed out a breath. "You."

"And I take what I want, when I want," he said.

"You want me," she said, wiggling her hips.

Her body brushed over his cock and he had to clench his teeth so he didn't groan.

"If you don't behave I might just go take a shower and jack off on my own," he said with a slap to her thigh.

Marissa's eyes widened. Gage wasn't sure if that was because of his words or the love tap. But he was going to find out.

"Roll over," he ordered.

She didn't waste any time turning onto her stomach, giving him the perfect view of her firm ass and flawless back and shoulders.

"Up on your hands and knees," he said.

Marissa lifted up and gave a wiggle of her hips.

Gage smacked her butt. "Don't get cocky," he said. "Or this will turn into a punishment."

When his hand had landed on her skin, she'd moaned.

He didn't know how he'd gotten so lucky to find a mate who enjoyed the same play that he did and could handle his dominant side, but Gage knew he was lucky.

"Now," he said, raising to his knees before her. "I'm going to claim every inch of you and you're going to remain perfectly still."

He had no doubt that he'd given her enough time to get control of her pleasure. He wanted her to enjoy every minute and now that he'd allowed the passion to cool a little he could make her hot again.

"Do you understand?" he asked.

"Yes, Gage," she whispered back.

"Good girl," he praised. He lifted his hand then let it drop down. The sound echoed around the room as his palm struck her flesh.

Marissa hissed but wiggled again.

"Stay still," he reminded her.

"Sorry."

She didn't sound sorry at all. He let his hand fly again, this time a little harder. He would never use his full strength against her even if she was a shifter. He had no intention of ever hurting her.

What Brandon had done was against every single thing that Gage stood for. An Alpha protected and cared for his Pack.

He couldn't think about that. Marissa deserved every inch of his attention.

On the fifth smack, Marissa was pushing back.

He stopped.

"No!" she wailed, dropping her head, panting.

"Don't move." Gage waited until she nodded before he began again.

Marissa remained frozen but her moans and gasps grew in volume. His cock was so hard that it was painful. But Marissa was responding so sweetly.

After twenty swats, Gage grasped his cock and moved to press against her pussy.

Still Marissa did not move.

"Perfect," he murmured, pushing in.

She sobbed, actually sobbed, and Gage withdrew before he slammed back in. Marissa would be able to feel him each time his hips hit her reddened ass. The pleasure-pain would keep her on the edge until he decided to let her come.

With a tight grasp of her hips, he pounded into her until it was even too much for her to follow his order and she was pushing back to accept him.

The familiar tingling at the base of his spine signaled his need for release so he reached around and fingered her clit hard.

Marissa screamed then her body clamped around his cock as they orgasmed together.

He was panting and shaking but managed to pull her gently to her side so that they could lie together. He stroked her arm basking in the afterglow. Marissa already had her eyes closed while he petted her. Gage cuddled her close, vowing to never let her go.

If he could protect her from having to ever see Brandon or his father again he would. He knew that his dad and the Council thought that facing those who'd hurt her would help Marissa overcome her past but Gage wasn't so sure. He really wished that he could take her away.

With a heavy sigh Gage settled further into the mattress as he tugged Marissa over him. All he could do was hold her while she faced her demons.

Chapter Eleven

The coffee was strong and sweet, which was a good help to start her day. Marissa was tired and out of sorts. The Council would arrive soon and she was nervous.

Gage glanced across the kitchen table at her when his cell phone rang. The sense of dread that filled her must have been shared by the others at the table since all conversation stopped. Or maybe they had been expecting the call. It wasn't like they had a reason to be afraid, after all.

"Excuse me," Gage said while standing up. He paced away as he swiped his finger over his phone. "Hello."

Marissa watched him as he strolled to the sliding glass doors then pulled one open. He closed it behind him but every shifter in the room leaned forward. They might be able to hear but she sure the hell couldn't. She'd just have to wait until Gage came back inside and told her what was going on.

Luckily it was a short conversation. He hung up the phone then turned around. His gaze met hers and he smiled. She nodded going to him as he headed back into the house. Marissa moved quickly so that her palm was in his and she felt the heat from his body when he held out his hand to her.

It was so nice to finally have someone to lean on. She'd always considered herself an independent woman but in reality she'd wanted someone to take care of her.

She'd never had that before and Gage was the perfect mate. He might be demanding and stubborn but she trusted him completely.

"The Council will be arriving soon," he said. "They've

already spoken to Brandon and his father and now want to hear our side of the story. I'll go first but after that they want to speak with you," Gage said to her.

Marissa nodded.

"Just remember that they're here to pass judgment on Brandon and his Pack. They can't and won't harm you. You are my mate. They accept non-shifters as they would a shifter or human. You're safe here."

How Gage knew what she was worried about she didn't know but Marissa was grateful. She was learning a lot about herself the more time she stayed with Gage. He'd brought up her non-shifter status several times but when he did it was never with disgust.

"I'll make sure the study is ready," Logan said. "I've been in meetings with the Council before and know how they like things." He rushed out of the room.

"It's going to be fine," Gage's father said, walking up to her. He lifted her chin. "You are our family and the Council is here to protect you and punish Brandon. I know these men that are coming today. Each one of them led their own Packs with love and caring. They will be horrified to hear how you were treated."

There was just so much happening, and so quickly, that Marissa actually felt somewhat light-headed.

"Would you like some air?" Cain asked from beside the door. "We could take a short walk in the back but stay close enough that you'll be available for when the Council needs you."

Marissa looked at Gage. She'd love to go outside but she didn't know how he'd feel about her being alone with Cain. She would never have given it a second thought before Gage but now she wanted to be considerate of his feelings.

"I think that's a great idea," Gage agreed.

"Come along then." Cain waved to the door.

Marissa lifted her face for a kiss from Gage. She'd thought it would be just a peck since the other two men were in the room but he wrapped his arms around her back and held her in tight before he plundered her mouth. She was panting and aroused by the time he pulled away.

"Just a reminder of who you belong to," Gage said.

Like she could ever forget. Her ass was still a little sore from him marking her the previous night. She knew her cheeks were red from blushing so she kept her head down and strolled through the door that Cain had opened.

The wood deck was solid as she walked carefully across it to the stairs. Once she was standing on the grass she stopped and closed her eyes.

The last time she'd done this was when she'd first made love with Gage. She'd felt like things were out of control then too. But now she had someone she could lean on, depend on. Marissa smiled before she took a deep breath.

She could handle the Council. Sure, she was nervous but the one thing she wasn't was weak. She'd grown up having to fight for herself and Elizabeth. Even though her sister was older she was also unable to stand up for them. Elizabeth just didn't have it in her. But Marissa could and did when she was able.

Now that she was the mate to an Alpha she had to call on that strength. Only Gage would be there for her and her for him. They could rely on each other and care for the Pack.

A Pack. In her heart Marissa had always wanted to belong but had never admitted it to anyone. Since she didn't think that she'd ever be accepted she couldn't deal with the letdown. Now she didn't have to.

She could make decisions about the Pack and help where needed. The biggest way she could think about being needed was to be there for other non-shifters. To make sure that no one else suffered as she had.

Maybe Gage's father could help her reach out to some of the other non-shifters. He'd said that he knew of Packs that had them.

Decision made, she opened her eyes and turned.

Cain sat on the top step of the porch peering out at the trees. When she moved he glanced over at her.

"Sorry," she said, embarrassed that she'd forgotten about him.

"No problem," he told her and stood. "You needed a break and fresh air always helps."

She nodded. "Yeah."

Cain smiled. "You remind me of someone from my Pack. You like to be seen as strong and independent but you need someone to care for you."

Marissa wasn't surprised Cain could read her. It was always the quiet ones that saw more than you wanted them to. "Is she special to you?"

Cain jerked back and she hid a grin. Oh yeah, she had his number right back.

"She's just a girl that I grew up around. She didn't have any family and my father made sure she was taken care of," Cain said.

Marissa could tell by the way his gaze darted around that Cain wasn't about to admit his feelings for this secret woman. "Where is she now?"

"Emily's enrolled in school," he said. "She wanted to go away and try to make it on her own, although she still comes back for all the big Pack events."

Yeah, if this Emily was attempting to make it without the support system of the Pack they did have a lot in common.

"I'd like to meet her someday," Marissa said. "It'd be nice to have some real friends."

"I'll make sure she's home the next time Gage visits. I doubt he'll go anywhere without you from now on," Cain said.

Marissa planned to make sure her mate never left her behind.

Logan appeared at the top of the porch. "They're ready for you, Marissa."

Damn, she guessed she'd spent more time in her mind than she'd thought. "Okay," she said. She rolled her shoulders back and lifted her chin. It was time to do what she needed to — she would not be intimidated.

Cain grinned at her as she passed and Logan dipped his head. Marissa strode forward and walked through the kitchen toward the center of the house. Gage had shown her where his study was before and she had liked the space, especially the warmth of the room with the heavy furniture and wood-burning fireplace.

She was glad that the Council had come to Gage's house. It was probably the place where she felt the most comfortable at the moment. Plus he'd be close by.

The house was quiet and Marissa hadn't realized how much that seemed wrong until just then. Logan had requested that everyone stay away while the Council was there, even sending Hannah off, so only her, Gage, Logan and Gage's dad occupied the house. She didn't even know when her sister was going to make it back. Gage had said that Logan was taking control of the travel plans and there was nothing she needed to worry about. Marissa was kind of happy about that. She felt guilty enough that Elizabeth and Greg's honeymoon had been interrupted that she didn't want to screw up getting them back into the territory.

There was a man she'd never seen outside the door and he smiled at her as she approached.

"You must be Marissa," he said, holding out his hand. "Congratulations on your mating."

"Uh, thank you," she responded.

"I'm Stephen, one of the Council's guards. I've known Gage since we were both small boys. I was so happy to hear he'd found you," Stephen said.

Marissa nodded even though she wondered how he could mean that when all of this was her fault.

"Go right in," he told her, waving toward the door.

"Thank you," she said, stepping past him. She turned around. "It was nice to meet an old friend of Gage's. I wish it was under better circumstances."

"Next time it will be," he said.

Marissa took a deep breath then knocked on the door. It opened and Gage stood there. He could still take her breath away with how handsome he was. He smiled and Marissa felt the urge to touch him. Luckily he reached for her, saving her from having to make a decision.

"It's going to be fine," he whispered against her brow while brushing his lips over her skin. "They're here to help."

Marissa peered up into his eyes. "I know," she said. "I'm strong enough to do this."

"Yes, you are," he agreed. "Now come."

Three men sat in a semi-circle in comfortable-looking chairs with cups of coffee on a table near them. They smiled then rose as she approached with Gage.

The hair on the back of her neck stood from the power in the room. Including Gage, the men were all Alphas and it was obvious to even her non-shifter senses.

"It's okay, dear," the closest Council member told her. "I'm Tim Babcock and these gentlemen are Alan Conrad and Andy Williams. We just want to take your statement, verify the events, and as we've spoken to Gage already he's welcome to stay."

Marissa let out a breath. She glanced over at her mate and he nodded. She didn't even have to ask and that helped her gain some of her much needed strength.

Gage led her to a couch located directly in front of the chairs where the Council Alphas were seated. They sat together and relief flooded her when Gage scooted closer and took her hand.

"We request that you tell us in your own words of what happened while you were in your birth Pack up to and including your sister's ceremony," Alpha Conrad said.

Marissa rubbed her free hand on her jeans. "I don't know where to start," she admitted.

"Wherever you think is best. If we need you to go back any we'll ask," Alpha Babcock said.

"Okay," Marissa said then started to tell them how she'd become close Brandon.

The story wasn't a short one but the three Council Alphas

paid her every bit of attention as she spoke. At one point Gage stood and got her a glass of iced water. She drank it down, feeling better as the cool liquid soothed her throat. She'd never spoken this much.

Alpha Babcock gave her a small nod so she started to speak once again.

Through the entire story Gage held her hand. She felt each time that he tensed when he didn't like what she was saying or he was having trouble handling it. If she wasn't so selfish Marissa wouldn't have made him stay. Instead she clung to him.

It was harder than she'd thought it would be, reliving her past. In the years that she'd been on her own, Marissa really thought that she'd gotten over what had happened. But a couple of times she teared up and Gage pulled her close.

"If you need a break we understand," Alpha Babcock said right after she'd explained about being kicked out of the Pack and the week she'd waited for Brandon.

"No," she told him. "I'd really like to get this over with."

"I understand," Alpha Babcock replied.

Gage rubbed her back and she took a deep breath then continued. The next part of being on her own was easier since she was proud of surviving. Even talking about coming there and meeting Gage was nice. She didn't elaborate on the fight that she and Gage had the morning of her attack. They didn't need to know that.

"So," she said. "That's about all there is."

Marissa felt drained and exhausted. She glanced at the clock above the fireplace and realized that she'd been in there for almost an hour. She collapsed against Gage, not caring what the Council Alphas thought about it.

"Did you get everything you need?" Gage asked.

His voice was rough and she could still feel the tension in his body.

"Yes," Alpha Conrad said. "Everything that Ms. Boyd told us matches the statements given by you and Brandon. Brandon didn't think he'd done anything wrong so he had no trouble recounting his story."

"So what's next?" Gage asked.

"We'll give our judgment to Brandon and his father," Alpha Babcock stated. "We've already appointed an Alpha to take over the Pack. Any members that are found to have been involved — and we are aware there are more — will be disciplined by the new Alpha."

"I didn't know you could appoint an Alpha." Gage sounded shocked.

"Only in extreme cases," Alpha Conrad said. "Most of the time we help an Alpha choose a replacement when they have trouble. Very few Alphas don't have a backup plan or someone already in the Pack that can become the Pack leader, but it does happen."

Gage shared a look with Marissa.

"Who would take over our Pack?" she asked him.

"Before we mated I appointed Logan. Now that's a decision we would make together," Gage said.

Marissa actually agreed with Gage's assessment that Logan would be a good Alpha. "I already agree with you."

He nodded.

"There is another matter we'd like to discuss with you both," Alpha Williams spoke for the first time.

Marissa stiffened, she couldn't help it. She didn't know if she could deal with anything else.

"We'd like to bring your father in, Gage," Alpha Babcock said.

Gage nodded before he pressed a kiss against her temple. "Remember we have each other. Everything is going to be okay."

She tried to give him a reassuring smile, she really did, but the dread that filled her was too strong. These men were Council Alphas and very powerful. She'd rather they just left and she and Gage could sneak back up to their room.

It was Alpha Williams who stood and went to the door. He was only gone a few minutes but it felt like an eternity. The other two Council Alphas spoke quietly. She had no doubt that Gage could hear them even if she couldn't. He didn't seem worried, but then again he was still upset over what she'd shared earlier so he was difficult to read at the moment.

When Gage's father entered behind Alpha Williams he was smiling. He crossed over to her and Gage and pulled her into his arms. Marissa was so shocked that she hugged him back automatically. Not only had he made a beeline straight for her but he was embracing her in front of the other Alphas. Her, a non-shifter, who was the cause of all this trouble.

"I'm very proud of you," he whispered to her. "It couldn't have been easy but you did what needed to be done to protect yourself and this Pack."

Marissa closed her eyes as she leaned on him. She didn't think she'd done anything special but it hadn't been easy. She appreciated his support.

"Now," he said before he drew back. "Let's finish up in here."

"Okay," she agreed.

When she turned to Gage to sit back beside him he was beaming at her. Really, the two of them were acting like she was some sort of hero. While it was nice, she thought they were being silly.

"I love you," Gage murmured as she rejoined him.

Damn, every time she heard those words she wanted to melt. "Me too," she whispered back.

"What can we do for you?" Gage asked the Council in his normal volume.

"I've been speaking to your father about what your mate and her sister have been through. We'll be speaking with Elizabeth when she arrives because I am very interested in how all this has affected her," Alpha Williams said.

"Elizabeth didn't do anything wrong," Marissa almost shouted as she tried to launch herself up off the couch.

Gage's arm around her stomach stopped her movement while pissing her off. She tried to push him away but he tightened his hold.

"Shh," he chided.

She sat fuming, and when Alpha Williams appeared amused, she had to literally bite her tongue.

"Of course she didn't," Alpha Williams said. "We are hoping that she can give us a point of view that we haven't tried to see before. As the sister or family member of a non-shifter we hope to offer them support as well as any non-shifter so that they may comfort and assist their non-shifter. We don't want to leave anyone out of aid we might be able to offer. Elizabeth could provide valuable insight."

Marissa flushed with embarrassment. One of these days she was going to learn not to jump to conclusions and make a fool out of herself. "Sorry," she mumbled, keeping her gaze on her lap.

"It's quite all right." Alpha Babcock waved his hand as he chuckled. "Your spirit is one of the traits that we admire about you. We believe you will need it as well to help other non-shifters."

"You really think I'll be able to help someone?" she asked.

Gage moved his arm from her stomach to back behind her neck. "If anyone can, it's you," he said.

She placed her hand on his knee and gave him a squeeze.

"We want to believe that any wolf shifter would contact us if they were in your shoes but we know that's not reality. The way we operate seems to keep us isolated. It's needed since we do have to make hard decisions that involve Packs. By having you available we think this avenue will really open a line of communication for non-shifters who may be suffering." Alpha Conrad leaned forward as he spoke to her and Marissa could see the sincerity in his eyes.

It meant a lot to her that they wanted to make sure no other non-shifters suffered like she had. "What is it that you want me to do?" she asked. "I don't know anyone from other Packs."

"That's where your mate and the Council come in," Alpha Williams said. "We'd like you to set up something where other Pack members can contact you. We'll send out a memo to all Alphas, plus as our representatives visit Packs they'll spread the word. I figure it'll take a couple of months but this is the first part of the plan. If it works we'll come up with more ideas."

"What about a group chat too?" Marissa suggested. "That way not only can someone talk to me but it will be a community of non-shifters."

"That's a great idea," Gage's father said. "I can help you set that up in the next couple of weeks."

Marissa nodded then looked at Gage. "I think I need to speak to my mate about our plans. Can we have some time to think about this?" Marissa really wanted to be involved in the project and it seemed like Gage also approved of the idea but she wanted to make sure Gage felt the same way.

"Of course," Alpha Babcock responded. "Alpha Williams is heading up the project but we'll all leave you our contact numbers and emails."

"Okay," Marissa said.

A knock sounded at the door and Gage's father rose. "I'll get it."

"You doing okay?" Gage asked in a murmur.

"Yes," she assured him.

"Greg and Elizabeth have arrived," Logan told Gage's dad.

Gage stood then offered her his hand. "Let's go get some coffee."

She glanced over at the Council Alphas and received a nod from Alpha Babcock. As she rose, Gage slid his hand up to her neck. He kept a hold of her, leading her out of the room.

In the hallway, Greg and Elizabeth were waiting.

"Marissa!" Elizabeth exclaimed rushing toward her.

She opened her arms and Elizabeth fit herself right into the embrace.

"I'm so sorry that your honeymoon got interrupted for this," Marissa told her sister.

"Are you kidding?" Elizabeth shrieked. "I was so pissed off that Greg didn't tell me about the attack."

"I'm fine and if Brandon hadn't done what he did things might not have worked out the way they have," she said with a glance over at Gage.

"Really?" Elizabeth peered between Gage and Marissa. "Does this mean I get my sister back?"

"You never lost me," Marissa assured her. "But this means that when you have kids I get to be the cool aunt living just a few blocks away."

When Elizabeth's eyes filled with tears, Marissa pulled her sister back into a hug.

"It's good," she murmured. "Everything is so good right now I may have you pinch me later just to be sure."

"After all this time," Elizabeth sobbed. "I didn't think you'd ever be really happy and now you are."

Marissa held one hand up toward her mate. They grasped each other. "Yes, it's really happening," she repeated.

Epilogue

The quietness in her condo seemed so foreign to her that Marissa had to actually stop and look around just to orient herself. It seemed like she'd been gone for years instead of just a couple of weeks.

"You okay?" Gage asked as he laid his palm at her lower back.

"It feels weird to be here," she admitted.

"I can't even imagine," he said.

He pressed his lips to her temple and she closed her eyes. Her entire life was changing because of the man who held her. They would pack up a few belongings that she wanted with her right away before hiring movers to bring the rest of her stuff to Texas.

"I know this is going to be hard for you. But our Pack is in Texas. We can't stay here."

Marissa slipped from his arms and strode toward her favorite window. The curtains were closed so she yanked them open to reveal the ocean that she'd become accustomed to looking out at every morning. This would be the last time that she peered from up high to watch as the world revolved. Now she was part of what was happening. She didn't have to hide any longer. She laid her palm against the glass and smiled. She was going home.

"Who's Chad?"

"Huh?" Pulled from her musing, she turned to face Gage.

He was scowling at her with a small piece of paper in his hand. "Who is Chad?" Gage's tone was hard.

"I give up," she said with a smile. "Who's Chad?"

Gage glanced down at the note he held. "Someone who

wants a repeat of the night the two of you shared. Who wants, and I quote, 'To fuck you through the mattress again'," Gage told her.

"Oh," she said stupidly. Now she remembered her last one-night stand that she'd had before she'd gone to Texas. Before she'd met Gage.

"Oh?" he repeated.

"What do you want me to say?" she asked. "He's a guy I fucked, one time He meant nothing to me then and even less now that I met you."

He narrowed his eyes.

"You knew I had a past before we got together," she said. If this was going to be a problem they needed to discuss things before she picked up her life and moved to Texas.

"Yes," he agreed before he blew out a breath. "I did but that doesn't mean I have to like it."

"Seriously, Gage?" she challenged. "We came here to move my stuff to your house, to be with your Pack, and you're jealous?"

"I'm not jealous," he snapped.

Marissa wasn't going to even respond to that lie. She merely lifted her eyebrows.

"Fine!" He threw his hands up in the air. "I'm jealous! I'm fucking pissed because no one should have ever touched you but me. You're mine!"

The thrill that went through her at his claim shouldn't have been there but it was. She loved the fact that Gage was so possessive of her.

"I am," she agreed.

Gage's shoulder slumped. Marissa walked over to him until she was pressing her breasts to his chest. He gripped her hips and pulled her even tighter.

"I love you, Gage. I might have given my body to Chad or other people but you are the one that I gave my heart to," she said, cupping his face.

He'd started to growl at the mention of other men but when she'd finished he laid his forehead to hers. "I'm not sorry that I love you as much as I do. But I am sorry that I yelled."

She laughed. "It's okay. I kind of like it when you're jealous."

Gage snorted. "Oh yeah?"

Marissa brushed her lips to his before pushing into him. Gage responded by wrapping his arms around her waist and lifting her up. She gasped but the sound was swallowed by Gage as he plunged his tongue into her mouth. Marissa dug her nails into his shoulders right before her back landed on the couch. Gage covered her body with her legs on either side of his. She lifted her hips to drag against his erection. She loved how hard he was for her.

"Gage," she panted.

"Mine," he declared with a growl. "I'll show you that you belong to me then I'm taking you home to *our* Pack."

"Yes," she hissed, still rocking. "That's what I want."

He attacked her neck with his lips and teeth. The tiny bites reminded her that Gage was powerful but careful with her. She pushed at the hem of his T-shirt to try to get at his naked back.

"Please," she begged when he pulled back.

Gage grabbed his shirt and tugged it over his head before he did the same to hers. His hands were warm when he cupped her breasts and she could feel the heat through the silk material of her bra. Her entire body was on fire and she needed him to claim her.

Marissa pushed up and reached around her back to unclasp the garment while Gage continued to knead her flesh. Next she yanked on the button of his jeans. "Naked, I need you naked."

He swatted her hands away and stood then pulled his jeans down his legs. Gage had to stop so he could toe off his shoes and socks. She had a great view of his ass when he bent over. She couldn't resist. Marissa leaned forward and took a gentle bite of his ass.

Gage yelped, spinning around. "You did not just do that."

"I think I did," she corrected. "It's such a fine ass."

He tried to look stern but the curve of his lips told her that she'd amused him. Gage trailed his fingers down her arm and she shivered. Just a slight touch and he could command her to do anything. Marissa was a slave to him and if he ever wanted to hurt her she'd given him more power than anyone else in her life.

"I would never hurt you," he murmured.

She had no idea how he could read her like he did. "You are the only one who can."

"I won't," he promised.

He finished undressing her and she laid passive while he did, just watching as he concentrated on getting her naked. When she was bared and trembling on the couch, he leaned over her. Marissa was done letting him take care of her. It was time to show him that they were in this together.

She launched herself up from the couch then tackled him to the floor. He grunted but made sure that he took the brunt of the fall. As she straddled his waist she grinned at him.

"I don't know why I thought you were just going to let me have my way with you," he teased.

"Me either," she replied.

"So now that you have me, what are you going to do?" he asked.

Marissa rocked forward so his cock brushed against her clit. "I think I can figure it out." She gripped his erection and pumped him several times.

Gage bowed up, pressing his cock into her hold. "Yes!"

"Not yet," she said then released him.

"Baby..."

Gage lifted his arms but she shook her head before grasping his wrists and holding them down.

Marissa slid down his legs until she was kneeling at cock level. She retook him in her hand but this time as she jacked him she lowered her mouth to the tip. Gage was still trying to push his cock deeper but she raised her head each time he attempted to push into her mouth.

He was growling and groaning, and Marissa knew she held all the power at that moment. Gage could force her to do whatever he wanted but she was safe with him. Instead, she was allowed to torture and tease.

When she was certain he couldn't take anymore before he lost his mind, Marissa went down and sucked him hard.

"Fuck!" he yelled while canting his hips.

She held the base of his cock then bobbed her head up and down until Gage was pleading with her. With her free hand cupping his balls, she could tell he was close to coming. Only when he was on the edge did she let go of him.

"No!" He almost screamed it.

Marissa didn't tease him anymore. She climbed on top of his lap and positioned his cock at the entrance of her pussy.

"I can't," he panted out. "I'm too close."

That was what she wanted, though. Marissa nodded at him while lowering herself down. He could take control now.

As soon as he was fully buried inside her, Gage flipped them over with his cock still deep. He started to thrust wildly. Marissa grabbed at any part of him that she could reach. Each powerful plunge of his sent them sliding across the floor, claiming her.

Gage might be close but so was she.

"Gage!" she yelled, climaxing.

"Love you," he said over and over until his strokes became erratic and he was coming.

The blood rushing in her ears was all she could hear and Marissa couldn't really see as her vision blurred.

"I can't feel my toes," Gage muttered, collapsing on top of her.

She grunted when his weight came down on her.

"We're going to have to get up eventually," he said, his mouth against her neck. "But I can't move."

Now that the passion had cooled, Marissa was finding the position they were in to be pretty damn uncomfortable. She wiggled under him. The floor was hard and cold.

Gage groaned. "Stop moving," he bitched.

"Can't," she said. "You should be on the bottom."

With a heavy sigh, Gage rolled off of her. That at least made breathing a little easier. "You need to help me up," she said. She turned her head to peer at him.

Gage blinked at her. "No, you help me up."

They laugh together. Finally Marissa managed to turn over and push herself onto her hands and knees. Gage eyed her with a smirk.

"Don't get any ideas," she demanded. "We are not going to have another round on the floor."

"I guess we could try to make it to the bed," he replied, smiling.

"Pack." She pointed a finger at him. "We need to pack so you can take me home."

He reached out and traced his thumb over her bottom lip. "I like the sound of that."

Marissa shook her head. Even after hot passion Gage always reverted back to sweet and kind. She climbed to her feet then held up a hand to help him. Gage gripped her as she pulled so he stood right in front of her.

She peered up at him, once again shocked at the changes in her life. When she'd left her apartment she'd been certain that she would come back, alone and sad. It hadn't been easy to get the nerve to visit her sister but thank God she had.

In her wildest dreams she hadn't ever thought that she would have a shifter in her condo helping her pack to move to a shifter territory. Marissa froze in place.

Dreams... She whirled around. The dream she'd had about the dominant wolf reminded her of Gage. She narrowed her eyes as he strolled around her apartment, glancing at her books and other mementos. She didn't have a lot but what she had filled her place with had meaning to her.

"What?" he asked, facing her.

No way. There was just no way she'd dreamed about Gage

before she'd met him. She was probably just remembering the wolf like him since her feelings were so strong.

Marissa smiled. "Nothing. Just admiring the view."

"Okay." He shrugged at her. "Should we start with your clothes?"

"Yeah," she agreed.

If she had enough clothes to get through until her other belongings arrived it should be fine. She already had the bag that she'd taken with her along with her laptop, iPod, and her other small stuff. The movers could take care of the bigger items. They would even box up what she wanted them to.

Gage stalked across the living room and into her bedroom. He stopped on the threshold. She'd done the room in black and whites with splashes of red. It was contemporary and sexy. At least she thought so.

"You're in charge of all our decorating," he said.

Marissa laughed. "I didn't think there was any room that needed to be decorated."

He turned to her. "Of course there is. We have to make the house our home. I haven't changed anything since I took over from my dad. I haven't really had the time but I also didn't have a reason to. Now I want to."

"Yeah?" she asked, pleased. She could already picture a few changes that she wouldn't mind taking care of. She liked his bedroom but she would think of something to add.

"Plus we need to get your office set up," he said.

"My office?" she questioned. She walked into the bedroom and opened the blinds so they had a little more light. She could enjoy the view while they worked.

Gage grinned. "We both know you're going to take the Council up on their offer to help with non-shifters. You'll need a place to work."

He was right. Marissa was excited to start helping the Council and other Packs support non-shifters. With Gage's help she really had something to offer with her experiences.

"The room next to my office is the library. I thought we

could move the books and furniture into the study. I know you like that room so I thought we could make it a little more comfortable. Also we can knock out the wall between my office and the library. We can make my office bigger and the other we'll set up for you," Gage said.

"That's…" What the hell could she say to that? Gage was willing to knock down walls for her. Change the house that he'd grown up in just to make her happy.

"Pretty great, right?" Gage supplied.

"Yes," she said while crossing to him. She lifted onto the tip of her toes to kiss him. "Thank you."

"You don't ever have to thank me," he said. "I would do anything for you. We're a team and I need you by my side."

"You don't think that we're still in danger? After the way the Council spoke I figured it was all over," Marissa said.

"It is," Gage assured her. "We're safe from Brandon and his Pack but that doesn't mean we won't run into any other trouble." He held her hand before he drew her to the bed.

They sat on the edge facing each other.

"What aren't you saying?" she asked.

"We've hidden who and what we are for a long time," Gage said. "One day our secret is going to get out. My father worried it would be during his reign as Alpha. Luckily that didn't happen. But I live with the fear that it will be under my time."

Marissa squeezed his hand. "If it happens I'll be by your side."

"That's all that I want," he whispered.

She wrapped her arms around his waist as she buried her face into his chest. It didn't matter what the future held. Marissa knew her place was by his side. They would help the non-shifters and protect the Pack. She was the mate of the Pack Alpha, after all. She had a responsibility to them and to her lover.

Pack Enforcer

Excerpt

Chapter One

Emily Black kicked her shoes off and watched as they flew across her living room. Godforsaken things. She hated shoes no matter what kind they were. At least the tennis shoes she wore to class were more comfortable than the heels her friends wore.

She kicked them under the coffee table as she passed and stripped off her shirt and jeans while heading into the bedroom for loose shorts and T-shirt. Once comfortable, she headed into the kitchen. The fridge, which she kept overstocked, was cool as she opened it. She grabbed a bottle of water and the Tupperware full of lasagne she had packed.

Heating it up in the microwave, she sat on the counter to wait for it with a fork in her hand. Many people would consider her behaviour weird or think that she hadn't eaten in hours. But, for her, it was just another day.

She had eaten lunch only two hours ago, but a shifter burned a lot of energy and needed to eat large regular meals.

She, however, ate many small meals. Especially around the few people she called her friends. Even though the world had finally admitted there were Shifter or Were creatures out there, she didn't like to call attention to herself. No one at school knew about her. Of that she was pretty sure. To them, she was just a quiet girl who liked to study and keep to herself. She was pretty in a traditional way, but not a head-turner. She would leave being stunning and charming to those around her. She preferred to blend in and not draw attention to herself.

She could see her answering machine light blinking, indicating she had a message, but wasn't in any hurry to check. It was probably someone trying to sell her something. She didn't get many phone calls.

* * * *

Cain knocked on the door to his Alpha's study and waited for the grunt meaning to come in. He entered and remained silent as Lamont finished his phone call. If Lamont hadn't wanted the conversation overheard, he wouldn't have let Cain in. Werewolf hearing was better than any device you could buy.

Cain immediately recognised the young Were's voice on the other end of the line. She spoke softly to the Alpha of the Pack, although her tone showed frustration. Hearing her voice sent a shiver down Cain's spine and a jolt to his cock.

They all worried about the young Were women who were out of the Pack's territory. In all of the attacks that had recently taken place, the females were away from home, out of Pack territory. Showing why he was Alpha, Lamont was calling them home before Cain had thought of it.

"Have some bags packed when your ride gets there," Lamont said sternly into the phone.

Cain barely held back a smile when he heard the order.

"No, someone will be there to pick you up." He looked over at Cain. "It will be someone you recognise from the Pack. Do not leave with anyone else."

Lamont listened for a few more minutes before cutting her off. "No. You will stay in one of the cabins. It will be fully furnished for your arrival." He waited again. "You'll stay until we know what is going on and I tell you it's okay to go back." That was all Alpha speaking to one of his Pack. Cain knew how Lamont felt about Emily. How everyone felt.

Emily had been changed as a child, which was against every rule and law they had. Most children could not handle the stress of change. That was why it was forbidden. Too many children had died back in the settling days before his family had a Pack leader. It was Lamont's father who had forbidden the change of children or anyone who did not choose it. There were too many risks.

Someone could carry the Were DNA two ways—through birth or by being bitten. However, being bitten did not mean they would automatically change. They must carry the strain somewhere down their line.

Cain's brother, Tony, could explain it better. Tony was a natural born talker. He could smooth over anything or anybody. He was the face of the Pack. When the Packs had decided to come out in the open, to stop hiding from the world, there needed to be a recognised face. A face that people could see and not think of a monster. Cain was just glad it wasn't him. He would rather stay home in his Pack's territory, keeping watch and protecting his Alpha.

He turned his attention to the man who sat behind the desk. A man he respected more than anyone else.

"Emily Black," Lamont told him once he hung up the phone.

"She's coming home?" Cain asked even though he knew

the answer.

Lamont nodded at him. "I want every female home and safe. Especially her."

Cain understood what Lamont was saying.

They had rescued her from the cage she had been put into after she had been changed — when the ones who had changed her couldn't handle her. She had been filthy and bruised from head to toe. Neglected and scared with no idea what was going on. She'd been twelve. Now, ten years later, she would be coming home to be kept safe once again.

"I want you to go get her and get her here safely," Lamont told him.

More books from
Crissy Smith

*Adam White is the new Alpha in his territory but Tasha
Johnson may the one in charge.*

The Rogue meets the Alpha…and their worlds explode.

A wolf and bobcat come together and change one community, forever.

A pack divided…brought together by love.

The shifter world has announced their presence…and now must deal with the consequences.

About the Author

Crissy Smith

Crissy Smith lives in Texas with her husband, daughter, and three Labrador retrievers. The three dogs love to curl up under her computer desk and nap while she writes. It doesn't leave a lot of room for her but what's a woman to do?

When not writing or reading, she enjoys hunting, camping and shooting. But she has a girly side too and is addicted to pedicures and coffee.

She has been writing since she was a teenager and still loves everything to do with the paranormal. Her stories and characters all have a place in her heart. She loves the alpha male, the dominant werewolf, or the Master vampire which find their way in most of her books.

Learn more about the characters she has created at her website where they have their very own page. It will be updated from time to time to let you know what's going on with them. Also you can find out who will be in the next book.

Crissy Smith loves to hear from readers. You can find contact information, website details and an author profile page at https://www.totallybound.com/

TOTALLY
BOUND

Home of Erotic Romance